Joss Wood loves books and travelling—especially to the wild places of southern Africa and, well, anywhere. She's a wife, a mum to two teenagers and a slave to two cats. After a career in local economic development, she now writes full-time. Joss is a member of Romance Writers of America and Romance Writers of South Africa.

Homecoming Heartbreaker

JOSS WOOD

MILLS & BOON

First published in Great Britain 2021
by Mills & Boon, an imprint of HarperCollins*Publishers* Ltd,
1 London Bridge Street, London, SE1 9GF

www.harpercollins.co.uk

HarperCollins*Publishers*
1st Floor, Watermarque Building,
Ringsend Road, Dublin 4, Ireland

Large Print edition 2021

Homecoming Heartbreaker © 2021 Joss Wood

ISBN: 978-0-263-29320-3

08/21

MIX
Paper from
responsible sources
FSC™ C007454

This book is produced from independently certified
FSC™ paper to ensure responsible forest management.
For more information visit www.harpercollins.co.uk/green.

Printed and bound in Great Britain
by CPI Group (UK) Ltd, Croydon, CR0 4YY

Dedicated to Karen Booth and
Reese Ryan, my smart,
talented, funny friends.
Working with you guys is always a blast.

One

Well, he was back.

Mack Holloway raked his hand through his black hair and rubbed his stubbled jaw, steering his Benz into the turnoff to the old logging road, a mile or so from the stone gates of Moonlight Ridge, the exclusive inn and resort owned by his adopted father, Jameson Holloway. This time he wasn't home for a one-night stay or a flying visit on his way to another city; he was here for a couple of months. And yeah, the thought made him grind his teeth and his throat tighten.

Mack cut the engine and pushed open his door, exiting his low-slung, stupidly expensive sports car. Slapping the door closed, he forced himself to look over the roof of the Benz to the thick forest of yellow pines. He swallowed, panic crawling up his throat. He didn't want to make the short walk up the road, to look at the place where his life had changed. He'd lost so much that night, his family, stability, *Molly*...everything that mattered.

Jamming his hands into the pockets of his pants, he forced his feet to move, feeling the cold fingers of a light mist touching his face. He didn't want to look at the scene of the accident but if he was going to be living here for the foreseeable future, then confront it he must.

Mack walked on and the mild spring wind lifted his hair and plastered his shirt against his chest and stomach. After a few minutes he stopped and looked around, realizing he was standing at the exact spot where the truck had left the road, and he swallowed, trying to ease his suddenly tight throat.

But instead of reliving that night from start to finish, as he expected to, he only recalled the screams, heard the high whine of the engine as the truck rolled.

He'd lost control of the truck and his temper. He'd failed to look after his brothers, Grey and

Travis. He was the oldest and they had been his responsibility.

It was one night, fifteen years ago, but it had had enormous ramifications. He'd thought himself invincible, they all had, but that night taught him that actions sometimes had massive consequences. As a result, he was rarely spontaneous and never made quick decisions. And keeping calm, rational and controlled was vitally important to Mack. It was his guiding principle, his compass point.

He couldn't change the past and the stupid decisions he made but he could control the present and plan for the future. To do that he needed to push the past aside and focus on the here and now…

On what he could control…

He was back in Asheville, temporarily returning to Moonlight Ridge because Jameson—the man who'd rescued him from the system shortly before his eighth birthday—recently spent a week in the critical care unit in Asheville's premier hospital after experiencing a brain episode.

They'd operated, Jameson was home, but the next few months would be critical to his long-term health. His adopted father's recovery was contingent on keeping his stress levels at a manageable level.

And Moonlight Ridge was the source of most of his stress…

On his way back to where he'd parked his car, Mack glanced to his right, knowing the boundary to Jameson's super luxurious resort, a smaller and more exclusive version of their neighbor, the famous Biltmore, was just a few miles to the north. Both properties were institutions in Asheville, North Carolina, and over the past seventy-five years Moonlight Ridge had been the retreat of kings and politicians, ultra-reclusive Hollywood celebrities and international billionaires.

And Jameson, as the owner and operator of the stunning stone-and-wood inn, had been the face of Moonlight Ridge for decades. He lived to work, and the luxurious resort where he'd raised them was his world. People energized him and he knew every guest by name.

But Jameson's individual attention to their guests was going to be, for the next six months at least, impossible.

After many tense and terse arguments with his brothers, and with Jameson himself, they'd finally come to a compromise: each of Jameson's sons would temporarily relocate to Moonlight Ridge. Mack, because he was the oldest—and despite knowing how hard it would be face Molly again—volunteered to take the first shift. It was the least he could do to try to atone for the devastation he'd caused…

Mack knew that complete atonement was impossible, but he had to make the effort.

But God, how he wished Molly wasn't still working as Moonlight Ridge's manager and living on site.

Mack placed his butt against the side panel of his car and stretched out his long legs, rolling his head to relieve the knots in his neck.

He met Molly even before he met Grey and Travis, his adopted brothers. He'd been eight and she, the daughter of Jameson's accountant, seven. He'd been entranced by her corkscrew blond curls, olive complexion and her fascinating light green-blue eyes.

Molly's complete lack of fear of Jameson, a big, burly, dark-skinned man—so different from his slightly built, mean-as-hell Korean biological father—helped him become accustomed to his new dad and his many rules and regs. With

Molly's help, he soon realized that Jameson was all bark and no bite. Over the next few months, he started to relax and then to thrive.

He had Jameson, he had Molly and he felt, *finally*, loved and secure.

Six months later Grey joined their little family and two months after him, Travis. They might not look the same, Jameson told them—Jameson and Travis were African American, Grey was white and Mack's father was of South Korean descent—but taking his name made them his, they were Holloways and they were a family. Diversity was strength, Jameson had told them; differences were to be celebrated and skin color was irrelevant.

Jameson, as he'd found out later, always wanted kids but never found the right woman to give him any. On hearing how difficult it was for older kids to find a forever home, Jameson scooped up Mack, a kid who lost his mother at childbirth and was abandoned by his dad when he was seven.

Mack knew how lucky he was. And, he figured, he couldn't have been that bad because Jameson went on to adopt two more boys close to his age.

That first year, with all three boys trying to find their feet and their place in their new family, was unbelievably tough. They all had trust issues, a fear of being disappointed, preferring to keep themselves to themselves. But Jameson kept a firm hand on the wheel and steered them through the storm, frequently reminding them that they were a family, and they'd better get used to the idea.

They listened and, despite not sharing a drop of blood nor a strand of DNA, became brothers in every sense of the word. For almost a decade he had a father and two brothers who, he believed, would go to war for him.

And he had Molly, his north star.

He supposed it was inevitable, given how close they were, that his and Molly's relationship would turn romantic, and those last four months they'd spent together had been the best of his life. They'd laughed, loved and explored their sexuality, convinced that they'd spend the rest of their lives together.

Then the accident ripped apart his family and lost him his oldest friend and his new lover…

After the accident, believing that he wasn't deserving of his family, of any type of love—

Molly's included—he'd left Asheville and everything he adored behind, cutting all ties with surgical precision. It was his way to punish himself and he'd been stunningly successful in doing just that.

For years he'd been a walking, talking emotional bruise.

Mack scrubbed his face with his hands, reluctantly admitting that, sometime after college, he could've approached her, made some effort to be, at the very least, polite. But no, because he was stubborn and stupid and, yeah, scared, he let the years fly by without contact and now he felt as alienated from her as he was from his brothers. If he'd reached out sooner, made the effort to connect earlier, their upcoming meeting would not be a fraction as awkward as it was bound to be.

Moonlight Ridge was Molly's home, probably more than it was ever his. She'd lived on the property as a child, worked for Jameson in her teens and was his father's favorite-ever girl, the daughter he'd never had.

And she was now the manager of Moonlight Ridge and, because he was going to assume Jameson's duties at the resort, he would be working closely with his ex-friend and ex-lover. The woman he'd thought he'd make his wife, the mother of the children he'd once wanted.

Completely fabulous.

Mack slid into his car, punched the start button on his dashboard, but instead of pulling away, he stared at the emblem on the end of his hood, feeling edgy, tense and very unlike the super-cool, controlled businessman he normally was. All he wanted to do was to return to Nashville.

Asheville, Moonlight Ridge, Jameson and Molly were all agents of change and he didn't want variations; he'd designed his life and liked it exactly as it was.

But he owed Jameson. He'd do anything for the man who gave him stability and love, security and a family, when he needed them the most.

But his past and present were about to collide...

More than ever, Mack needed to stay in control.

Molly Haskell stood at the window of her third-floor office, her eyes on the long drive-way. She'd had a brief message from Mack, telling her he'd arrive this morning, and she cursed her elevated heart rate and dry mouth.

He'd left fifteen years ago; surely, she should be over him by now. Molly, frowning at the thought, gave herself a mental head slap. She was over him; *of course* she was. She refused to be anything *but* over him.

But Mack's return to Moonlight Ridge as Jameson's stand-in was going to complicate her business life—she refused to let him affect her or her emotions!—and put a hitch in her plans to revitalize the resort.

Just before he fell ill, Jameson promised to listen to her proposals to make the resort the premier destination in the South, but before they could meet, he collapsed and was rushed to the hospital, unconscious. His brain episode— another word for his narrowly avoiding an aneurysm—scared her senseless and all she'd been able to focus on was whether he'd recover or not. Now that he was out of danger, she could give her attention to Jameson's beloved business.

He was her mentor, her second father, the man she adored, loved and trusted and there was nothing she wouldn't do for him, including reviving his resort.

But as Moonlight Ridge's manager, she'd didn't have the authority, financial or otherwise, to make dramatic and sweeping changes. She'd now have to—*ugh*—get permission to implement her plans from, according to Forbes, one of the country's most brilliant young businessmen, Jameson's oldest son, Mack Holloway.

And Mack, because he was a leader not a follower, a visionary who liked to forge his own path, was bound to poke many holes in her plans.

Molly released a low growl, then a hard sigh. She was already annoyed with him and he hadn't yet arrived.

No, that wasn't true; being annoyed with Mack was her default setting. She was simply more annoyed with him than usual.

"I will not let him stand in my way."

"Talking to yourself again, Mol?"

Molly turned to see her best friend stepping into her small office. They'd met when they were ten or eleven, when Autumn's wealthy family vacationed at the resort two years in a row. When she didn't return for the third year, they exchanged postcards until their friendship faded in their early teens. Two years ago, a scandal involving Autumn's father—a famous Hollywood producer—chased her out of LA and she landed at Moonlight Ridge as their independent wedding planner.

Their friendship sparked again and these days Autumn ran all their weddings and events on a shared profit basis, and also arranged functions throughout Asheville as an independent contractor.

Autumn pushed her black glasses up her nose and joined Molly at the window, placing a hand between her shoulders. "Are you okay?" she quietly asked.

Of course she was. Maybe.

Molly stared at the Degas print on the opposite wall. The ballerina wore a frothy tutu, was on pointe and tilting down. In her teens Molly had been a talented dancer, one with a lot of promise, but she'd lost her beloved ballet that long-ago summer, along with so much else.

"Not really," she quietly admitted. Turning, she placed her bottom on the wooden window-sill and shrugged. "I'm hurt that, despite having worked here my entire life except for college, Jameson feels the need to bring in his sons to oversee operations."

"Maybe Mack will be too busy with his own work to get involved," Autumn suggested.

Hope flared in her chest. "Maybe. Maybe the brothers just told Jameson they'd stick around to get him to take it easy. You know how implacable he can be."

Molly tipped her head up to stare at the decorative ceiling in her office, trying to make sense of her mixed emotions. She was worried about Jameson, feeling nervous to be meeting Mack again after a fifteen-year absence, irritated that she wouldn't have free rein to manage Moonlight Ridge her way and terrified that Jameson's long-absent son would come in and tip over her carefully arranged apple cart.

"Am I allowed to still be angry that Mack dumped me?" Molly asked Autumn because, yeah, she was.

Autumn frowned. "Molly, it's been a long time. You were kids. Ninety percent of teenage relationships end."

Sure, but Mack had been so much more than a teenage fling. Before he'd become her boyfriend and her first lover, he'd been her best friend. Her refuge, the *one* person, besides Jameson, who had her back.

His leaving, without a word or explanation, eviscerated her. The months following his departure had been the loneliest of her life and contributed to her making the worst decision of her seventeen or so years, a mistake that still haunted her today.

"Talk to me, Mol," Autumn said.

What could she say? Autumn knew that Molly's father was Jameson's treacherous CFO. She knew Molly's history with Mack. How Molly and her family were forced to leave Moonlight Ridge when she was thirteen but how this place held everything and everyone she cared about.

But Autumn did not know about her *crime.*

"Mack and I working together is going to be awkward, uncomfortable. Mack has been home to visit Jameson before but, despite me living and working on the property, he's never sought me out to apologize for dropping out of my life, for not replying to the million text and email messages I sent him, the frantic voice mails I left on his phone."

Molly would never forgive him for treating her like she was disposable, like she was an object that he'd used and no longer valued.

She had her family for that.

There was something to be said for growing up. These days she was confident, assured, assertive and ambitious. She straightened her shoulders. "But I can handle Mack Holloway."

"Good. How?" Autumn asked.

He'd be expecting an attitude, Molly realized. He'd be prepared for a tirade. As a child and teenager, she'd expressed every thought, wore her heart on her sleeve, and Mack would expect her be as she was before.

Molly refused to be predictable. "I'm going to treat him as if he were any other employee, any other boss," Molly told her friend. "I'm going to be polite, friendly but distant and, above all, professional."

Autumn's arched eyebrows lifted. "And you think you can do that?" she asked, sounding doubtful.

Sure she could. She hoped. Trying to look, and sound, confident, Molly nodded. "It'll be a piece of cake."

Autumn patted her shoulder. "Well, you're about to find out, sweetie, because there's a car coming down the driveway."

Go time.

Molly returned Autumn's hug, sucked in a

deep breath, left her office and headed for the tight, small and prosaic servants' staircase. The old, sprawling mansion—with two large wings added to house many guests—sported a massive, imposing staircase, but the staff needed to be discreet and that meant flying up and down the narrow staircase at the back of the house.

Molly used one of the many secret passageways—in the 1930s the original owners ran a speakeasy for their wealthy friends and used the secret tunnels to stash their illicit booze—and slipped into the imposing hallway/lobby via a discreet door. Waving to Harry, who manned the front desk, she walked through the hall dominated by the magnificent staircase and stopped to shove a tulip back into a bountiful arrangement of fresh flowers.

Moonlight Ridge was Jameson's, but, emotionally, it was hers, too. She came back to work for Jameson after college because she'd felt so damn guilty—she still did—but these days there was no place she'd rather be than within the walls of this thick building, with its antiques and silver, art and antiquities. She loved the luxurious rooms, the ivy covering parts of the building, the extensive, lush grounds and the gorgeous lake that was a centerpiece on the property.

Molly stepped outside and watched as the matte-black, low-slung sports car made its way up the long, tree-lined driveway. Molly scowled at the wide-shouldered shadow behind the wheel.

Mack was back…

She gulped.

She'd moved on; she *had*. She hadn't spent the past fifteen years pining, for God's sake! There had been other men, not many, but she'd dated. But no one managed to capture her heart. To be fair, she hadn't allowed her heart to be captured. She was perfectly content to be single.

Besides, she'd rather avoid the drama men brought to her life, thank you very much.

Mack pulled to a stop and cut the growly engine to his car. Molly sucked in a deep breath and put her hands behind her back, her fingers tightly interlocked. She hoped she was portraying her polite, friendly "Welcome to Moonlight Ridge" face but she couldn't be sure.

This was, after all, the man she still wanted to run through with a rusty pitchfork.

Chill, Molly. It all happened so very long ago.

Mack stepped out of his car and Molly slammed

her teeth together to keep her tongue from falling to the floor. At eighteen, Mack had been gangly, all long limbs and unruly hair, a little awkward and uncoordinated. That wasn't something Mack needed to worry about now.

Molly tipped her head to the side and considered the man who'd been the center of her world so long ago. The boy she knew was gone and he was now a man, in every way that counted. His once shaggy hair was now expertly cut and styled, as black as a night in the Carolina woods. He'd inherited his Korean father's looks, his eyes—a deep, dark black-brown—and the shape of his face hadn't changed, but the light, sexy stubble on his jaw and chin was new.

But it was his body that had undergone the biggest change. He'd hit six foot two in his early teens but he'd always been skinny. He'd bulked up, his shoulders were broader, his thighs bigger, his chest wider. His shirt hinted at huge biceps and the wind slapped his white shirt against a stomach that was flat, hard and, she was convinced, ridged with muscle.

Mack, it was obvious, worked out. Hard and often.

Yum.

Molly felt the heat between her legs, the tingles in her nipples, and swallowed, looking for moisture in her mouth. *Yum? Really, Haskell?* He was a great-looking guy and, *rats*, she was still as attracted to Mack today as she'd been when she was a teenager. But unlike that naive, trusting girl she'd been, she now knew that there was a chasm between sex and love, that the two didn't normally have to walk hand in hand. She could appreciate a good-looking man; it was just conditioning and biology. Molly knew that she, and every other woman in the world, was hardwired to look for the strongest, best-looking mate, the one with excellent genes to give to her children.

She'd grown up, thank God, and it took more than a hot bod and gorgeous face to impress her these days.

Mack took his time acknowledging her and when he finally turned to look at her, his face was as imperturbable as she hoped hers was. "Hello, Molly."

God, even his voice was deeper, sexier, like well-aged red wine.

Molly inclined her head and didn't move from her position, annoyed to realize that her knees were now, and suddenly, the consistency of Jell-O. "Mack."

Mack placed his hands in the pockets of his pants—black, designer—and walked around the hood of his car to stand at the bottom of the steps. He looked up at her, his eyes shuttered. "I'm on my way to see Jameson…anything I should know before I head over there?"

Molly understood his asking; he knew she and Jameson were tight. Molly lifted one shoulder. "He's irascible and demanding. He fired another nurse this morning."

Frustration flickered across Mack's face. "That's how many now?"

"Nurses? One this week. Two last week."

Mack pushed a broad hand through his slightly wavy hair. "He needs a nurse, Molly. He can't be on his own."

Molly heard the accusation in his voice and bristled. "Hey, I'm trying to run the resort as well as keep an eye on him. There's only so much I can do but I did persuade his current nurse to stick around until you arrived today. He needs to accept help or, better yet, you find someone to nurse him who won't buckle when he yells."

"He doesn't mean it. He's just frustrated."

Molly scowled at him, annoyed that he was lecturing her about the man whom she'd known and adored all her life and worked with since she left college. The man she'd, sadly, betrayed a few months after Mack left Moonlight Ridge and Asheville.

Don't think about that now, Molly.

Irritated that she'd let him get to her, she forced herself to smile. "Did you have a good trip?" she asked, her tone completely, to her ears at least, false.

"Do you really care?"

Not a whit, she thought, keeping her smile in place. His eyes narrowed as he tipped his head back to look up, taking in the three-story stone building, covered in thick ropes of ivy. Like her, he'd grown up in shadow of this stone-and-wood building. He in Jameson's house a short distance away, she, until she was thirteen, in the manager's house situated beyond the orchard at the back of the property.

A picture of a young Mack, maybe eight or nine, looking up at the mansion in the same way—bemused and impressed, as if he was wondering what he was doing here—flashed on her brain's big screen. She'd often seen it on his face over the years, as if he still couldn't believe he got to call Moonlight Ridge home.

"Are you moving into Jameson's house?" she asked Mack.

Mack looked like he swallowed a sour lemon. "Since he doesn't have a nurse, I suppose I, temporarily, have to."

Molly narrowed her eyes at him. When they were kids, Mack had hung on Jameson's every word, and Jameson hadn't been shy to tell, and show, them how much he loved his sons. He'd been tough but fair. As one of Jameson's longest employees—she'd worked for him temporarily since she was fourteen years old and permanently since she was twenty-two—she'd seen how the feud among the brothers impacted her boss. Jameson managed to still be the consummate host, the charming innkeeper, but Molly saw him in his unguarded moments, and his sadness had been tangible.

And, okay, she was being a bit fanciful here, but Molly was convinced that Jameson's moods affected the inn. When Jameson felt upbeat and buoyant the mansion seemed to glow, its windows, always clean, sparkled and the ivy danced.

It seemed to shimmer, radiating his vivacity. When Jameson felt despondent or angry, the inn seemed to shrink in on itself, the stones seemed colder and the wooden frames, and doors, appeared dull.

To Molly, the inn was another character, the mad, rich, *adored* geriatric aunt everyone ran circles around. Well, she and Jameson did; the three Holloway boys left them behind a long time ago. Like Jameson, she didn't want to live anywhere else but here. One day, when Jameson heard what she'd done, she would have to leave, but today wasn't that day.

"A nurse I am not," Mack said, yanking Molly back to their conversation, "but spending some time together will give us a chance to catch up."

Molly gestured to the ornate doors behind her. "I need to get back to work and I'm sure you want to see Jameson. I'd appreciate it if you could take over the search for another nurse for him. Maybe you'll find someone who'll stick around."

Because he, sure as hell, wouldn't.

Two

In her messy office, Molly heard a rap on her partly open door and wearily lifted her head. Perfect. Just one more person she didn't want to see...

With her tiny build, waist-long blond hair and bright blue eyes, Beth looked like an angel, but Molly knew her brother's girlfriend was manipulative, demanding and self-absorbed. She fit into the Haskell clan really, really well.

"What do you want?" Molly asked her, her voice flat. Six months ago Grant demanded she find Beth a job at the resort and she'd handed her CV to Jameson, hoping and praying nothing came of it. Beth's résumé wasn't overly impressive but she had, apparently, bookkeeping experience, and Jameson hired her.

The books had been a mess before and Molly knew that Beth had made a bad situation considerably worse.

Before Jameson's collapse, Molly had expressed her concerns to him and he'd promised to look into the situation. If Molly had her way, she'd fire Beth but the hiring and firing of senior staff started and stopped with Jameson, and she didn't have the authority.

Great news for Beth; bad news for her.

"I heard that Mack Holloway has arrived."

Molly just stared at her, hoping to keep her expression bland. "If you've stepped in here to make asinine observations, you can just leave."

"I know that you and Mack had a thing way back when but if you are thinking of confiding in him, I would caution against it."

Molly rubbed her temples with the tips of her fingers, conscious of the headache building behind her eyes. A month or so back, tired of hauling around guilt and remorse—and after discovering her brothers took the money she'd recently given her mother to pay the gas and water bill and lost it playing blackjack—she'd, once again, told her family she was done and that they were on their own.

On hearing that she'd no longer fund their irresponsible lifestyle, her mom cried and told her she was unkind and a bad daughter. Vincent informed her that she could spare the cash; she was single, was being paid a mint and she owed them. Grant put his hand through the wall of the living room.

And when they calmed down, they did what they always did; they resorted to blackmail. If she didn't do as they asked, they'd tell Jameson she stole two thousand dollars from him when she was a teenager. They'd also imply that she hadn't stopped stealing from him, that she was more like their father than he ever imagined.

Jameson fired her accountant father for embezzling more than a hundred thousand dollars from him to fund his blackjack habit and charged him with theft. With her dad out on bail, Jameson gave them two weeks to vacate their house and the day the movers arrived, her dad dropped to the floor. Her last memory of her father was watching him leave Moonlight Ridge in an ambulance.

After his death, and despite the scandal, Jameson allowed the Haskell family to remain in their house on the grounds. It had been a wonderfully kind, magnanimous gesture but her mother and siblings never saw it that way. After her dad's death, Molly vividly recalled many conversations between Jameson and Vivi: him asking for her to exert some control over her rebellious older brothers, her blaming Jameson for her husband's death on the stress of being fired and facing prison.

After a series of incidents involving her brothers—skinny-dipping in the lake, playing their music far too loud, their harassing some VIP guests—Jameson insisted they leave the property. Despite being thirteen, Molly fully understood why Jameson didn't want any of the Haskells around. She couldn't blame him; she never wanted to be around her family, either.

Weeks ago, knowing that there was only one way to end this cycle of blackmail—and tired of living with her family's threats, with her burning secret, with the heavy guilt—Molly resolved to find the courage to tell finally Jameson the truth. She had the money to pay Jameson back, with interest, and if he fired her, well, she'd reluctantly accept his decision.

Being canned and being cut out of his life was no less than she deserved.

But Jameson collapsed before she could confess.

Now, because Jameson had to avoid stress at all costs, her confession would have to wait. She'd also considered moving Beth to another position within the resort but that meant hiring another bookkeeper and she didn't have the authority to do that.

No, the best course of action was to let Beth continue in her role, keeping her on a short leash and scrutinizing her work. And she'd keep funding her family until Jameson was stronger and could handle stress better.

Molly stared at Beth, not bothering to conceal her loathing. "You do realize that this is blackmail, right?"

Beth shrugged. "You shouldn't have threatened to stop helping your family."

Molly slapped her hand on her desk, her temper bubbling. "My brothers are older than me and haven't held down a job, ever. My mother has never held down a job for more than three months. Why should I help them?"

"Because Jameson pays you a ridiculously inflated salary and you can afford it," Beth replied, looking nonchalant.

"Jameson pays you a good salary, too!" Molly pointed out.

"They are your family and my money is mine."

Molly felt the old, oh-so-familiar wave of frustration. "When Jameson is better, I will tell him what I did. He'll probably fire me and I'll be out of a job. And the free ride will come to an end for all of you."

Beth had the audacity to smile. "You don't have the guts to cut them off, Molly. If you did, you would've divorced yourself from your family years ago. No, you still think they are going to snap out of this slump and you are all going to be a family and sing 'Kumbaya' around the fire."

Molly dropped her eyes, knowing that Beth had nailed her biggest wish, her secret desire for a loving and supportive family. Her mom had never been there for her—she didn't think Vivi even liked her much—and her brothers were consistently unreliable. She didn't need a psychologist to tell her that part of the reason she attached herself to Jameson, and his family, was her need to be part of a unit that loved and valued her. In Jameson she had a father figure and a mentor, Travis and Grey were her brothers, and Mack? Well, she'd thought she'd have her own family, the family she'd always wanted, with the oldest Holloway son.

Dead wrong there, Haskell.

Molly looked up and met Beth's icy eyes.

"The ball is yours to play, Molly. Don't confide in your old boyfriend, keep paying the family's bills and none of us will tell Jameson. He might or might not believe us but either way, it will upset him and we don't want that, do we?"

No, they definitely didn't.

Beth sent her another mocking smile and Molly considered throwing a stapler at her head. But before she could finish the thought, Beth stepped back into the hall and glided away.

Holy crap, could this day get any worse?

An hour later Mack stood outside Molly's office door and instead of knocking and entering, he took a moment to look at his onetime best friend, his first love. She was still as slim as she'd been at seventeen, with impossibly long legs, rounded hips and breasts that once fitted his hands perfectly.

Move your eyes up, Holloway.

Molly's body was world-class but her face still had the power to stop him in his tracks. Her grandfather was from Cuba, her mother's family had Scandinavian roots and she was a mixture of ethnicities. Her hair was still a riotous mop of blond, tight curls and he loved her sun-kissed, clear, gorgeous skin. Her nose was long and straight, her mouth wide, with a full sexy bottom lip he'd loved to nip.

But it was her eyes that always had the ability to drop him to his knees. They were a curious color, sometimes an aqua-blue, sometimes a light, direct green, sometimes a combination of both and touched with silver. The ring holding in all that color was a deep, dark blue, close to black, and her lashes were dark, long and thick. Her eyebrows, shaped and dark, were perfectly arched.

He'd loved her once, intensely, crazily. Fifteen years ago she'd been the reason why the sun rose and set, why birds flew and waves crashed. She'd been all that mattered.

That all changed the night of the accident and, last night, he'd spent many hours last night recalling every detail of that night from hell.

And, as always, he couldn't forget that it was

his biological dad's voice he heard as the wheels of his truck left the road. *You killed your mom and now your brothers might be dead, too. Leaving you was the best decision I ever made!*

The memories hadn't faded, not even a fraction. The storm had been wild and wicked, both inside the truck and out. Grey sat next to him on the bench seat of his F-150; Travis had been next to the door. The wind rocked the vehicle and his wipers battled to keep up with the pounding rain, and his headlights barely cut through the darkness. Travis was pissed that he and Grey hauled him away from his then girlfriend and hadn't stopped bitchin' since they left the restaurant's parking lot. He'd told Travis to shut the hell up, that he was trying to concentrate on the road but, instead of silence descending, Grey, normally the peacemaker, added gas to the bonfire when he ripped into Travis.

The combination of low visibility, speed and temper caused him to miss the curve of the road. Someone had been yelling as the truck became airborne and the right-hand side of the vehicle slammed into the side of the ravine.

And it was all because he'd lost control; he'd acted without thinking. He'd almost killed his brothers and while he and Grey escaped with minor injuries, Travis shattered his leg, lost his football scholarship to a prestigious college and had to rethink his life and make new plans.

When he lost control, bad things happened. And the person most able to make him lose control was Molly. And that was why he walked away from her, without a word or explanation.

To Mack, love meant losing control, and he was damned if he'd ever let that happen again.

Mack rubbed his chest above his heart and hauled in some air, remembering that a few years after he'd made peace with Jameson, he'd come home to visit his dad and, feeling cocky, decided to end the years of silence between him and Molly.

They weren't, he reasoned, kids anymore and they could put the past behind them. Shortly after arriving home on a fantastically hot Saturday in July, he'd gone in search of her and eventually tracked her down to the pond on the far northwest boundary of the property.

They used to make the walk often, crossing the steel-covered bridge and taking an overgrown path through a small copse of trees to the little lake. The guests never made it to the pond; the trail wasn't well marked and he, Molly and his brothers considered the pond to be their private swimming hole. It was where they built their treehouse, where they'd camped out under the stars.

He recalled approaching the pond from the trees and she'd been standing on the bank, dressed in a small bikini, poised to dive into the water. He instantly swelled in his shorts, desperate to reach her and haul her into his arms, thinking they could make love on her towel, in the sunshine. The need to have her, taste her, to make her his again had been overwhelming.

Memories collided with lust and he recalled the plans they'd made, the house they were going to build, the kids and dogs they were going to adopt, the life they were going to lead. The longing that swept through him at lost dreams and unfulfilled wishes caused his knees to liquefy, and he placed his hand on the nearest tree trunk to keep his balance.

Molly made him lose control and because control was *all* that was important, he turned around and walked away, determined to embrace his life of surface-based relationships and being responsible for only himself.

Subsequently, he'd only come back to Moonlight Ridge for flying, in-and-out visits. But now he was stuck in Asheville, overseeing the resort for two months or so. When his time was up, he'd hand over the responsibility to Grey. Or to Travis.

But in the coming weeks, he needed to talk to and interact with the manager of the hotel.

And that person was Molly.

Crap.

Mack rubbed his hand over his face and told himself to get a grip. He was here to do a job and nothing would be accomplished by his standing in the hallway outside her office.

Time to stop thinking about the past and get to work, Mack told himself and rapped on her door. Her head shot up and those sexy eyebrows lifted in surprise. Then her eyes widened and she stood up abruptly, pushing her chair back so hard that it slammed into the credenza behind her desk. "Is it Jameson? Is he okay?"

"Why wouldn't he be?" Mack asked as he stepped into her chaotic office.

"You have a weird expression on your face."

He'd thought he'd perfected his implacable expression but obviously not. Damn. "Jameson is fine, Molly. I checked in on him and he's asleep. I thought sleep was more important than letting him know I was here, so I didn't wake him up."

Molly closed her eyes, her expression one of pure relief. When she opened them again, she looked puzzled. "Okay, good. Then what can I do for you?"

"As you know, the only way we could get Jameson to take time away from the business was if one of his sons came home to oversee the resort while he is recuperating."

Molly's curls bounced as she nodded. "But I'm here so you don't need to bother," she said. "I'm perfectly capable of running this place on my own. You can concentrate on your own businesses."

Mack steeled himself to burst her bubble. "Jameson was adamant that there's too much for you to do and manage on your own."

Mack saw dismay and hurt flicker in her eyes before they iced over. "He doesn't trust me."

Now that was just stupid. Jameson trusted Molly almost as much as he trusted them. "Stop feeling sorry for yourself," he snapped, "and think."

He ignored her sharp, annoyed intake of breath.

"This place is enormous and Jameson has always had a pack of managers. Now it's only you. Why is that?" Mack demanded.

He saw her hesitate and watched as she looked for a reason that would placate him. Mack hoped she wouldn't lie.

Molly held his eyes for a minute but then all that stunning blue slid away. She dropped into her chair and pushed her curls off her forehead and out of her eyes. "I'm not sure what you mean, Mack."

"If you don't then you shouldn't be the manager of this hotel," Mack stated, keeping his voice cool.

Molly muttered a curse too low for him to hear. Gesturing to the chair, she ordered him to take a seat. "Okay, do you want the truth?"

"I always want the truth, Molly."

She didn't even bother to hide her skepticism at that statement. "Sure you do." Before he could ask her what she meant by that low, bitter statement, she told him about rising costs and falling income. The resort was unfashionable, needed updating, it was cash strapped and the guest occupancy was too low to sustain the business. She also informed him that the room decor was outdated and the food served by the kitchen was good, but not great.

Well, at least she wasn't looking at Moonlight Ridge through rose-colored glasses.

"Also, I think there's a perception out there that this place is for people of a certain age, so younger people with money don't come here," Molly added.

"And have you any ideas on how to turn that around?" Mack asked. Talking business with her was a lot easier than delving back into the past but he wasn't a fool; at some point they'd discuss why he left without saying goodbye.

But since she was treating him like he was just another business consultant or colleague, maybe he'd dodged that bullet. He hoped. And prayed.

Molly bent sideways, yanked open a drawer and pulled out a file, which she slid across the desk to him. "Actually, I do. I've spent an enormous amount of time working on a proposal to revitalize the resort. Jameson and I were going to dissect our business model, reconsider our marketing strategy and look at ways to cut costs. But then he got sick."

Mack tapped his finger on the glossy cover of Molly's file. "I'll read it as soon as I can and we can have that discussion you were going to have with Jameson."

Molly sent him a scathing look. "I'll believe that when it happens."

Yeah, there was no ignoring her sarcastic tone. "I don't lie, Molly. If I say I'm going to do something, I do it."

Molly shoved her chair, stood up and walked over to the window, folding her arms across her chest. "Forgive me if I don't trust anything you say, Holloway."

Mack gripped the bridge of his nose. So they were going to go there here and now. Oh, joy.

He'd apologize and then they could put this behind them and, hopefully, move the hell on.

He mentally tested a few sentences and when none of them felt right, he settled for simple. "I'm sorry I left you without saying goodbye, Molly."

She didn't respond for a long time and when she finally looked at him, he saw one raised eyebrow, a sure sign of her displeasure.

"That's it? One measly sorry?"

Mack lifted his hands, knowing he was on unstable ground. He recognized the temper in Molly's eyes; it burned as brightly as it did the day her brothers put a frog down the back of her dress.

"So no apology for not contacting me to let me know that you were okay? No sorry for not giving me an explanation, for dropping me from your life, for treating me like I was disposable? We were friends first, Mack! You don't treat people like you did but you especially don't treat your oldest friend like that!"

A wave of shame, hot and acidic, broke over him, and Mack closed his eyes, wishing he were anywhere but here. He wanted to be back in Nashville, in his office, or at one of his many breweries, talking about dry hopping and fermentation, yeasts and yields. He didn't want to be here, doing this.

Mostly because she was right. He'd treated her badly and his only excuse, if there was one to be had, was that he felt that he didn't deserve her; he didn't deserve anything good in his life. Giving her up had been one more way to punish himself.

It had also been a way to take back control. Love, in all its forms, was uncontrollable.

"I'm sorry I hurt you." What else could he say?

Molly turned slowly and her direct gaze pinned

him to the chair. "But you're not apologizing for leaving me alone, for running, for not having the decency to say goodbye face-to-face."

He couldn't tell her that if he'd done that then he wouldn't have left. If she'd asked him to stay, he would've because he'd loved her so damn much.

He'd failed his brothers and father. He didn't deserve her love, to have a family. It was far, far easier to be alone.

That was a truth he freely admitted, but only to himself.

Molly slid her hands into the pockets of her black pants, her expression remote. She nodded to the door. "I'm sure you want to unpack, get settled. While you do that, I'll get a housekeeper to dust and air Jameson's office, which, as you know, is right next door. It hasn't been used for a few weeks."

Subject closed, Mack thought. Thank God.

Mack nodded. "Thanks, M."

Mack winced at her old nickname. Jameson used to call them M&M when they were very young and the name stuck. But they weren't eight and seven anymore, and if he was going to work with Molly, he needed to keep things professional.

Before she could lambaste him for being over-familiar, Mack changed the subject. "When Jameson wakes up, I will talk to him about him firing his nurses."

Molly looked skeptical. "And you think that will help?"

His dad was as hardheaded as a concrete block so…no. Not really. "I can only try. Maybe he has an idea of whom he wants to nurse him."

"Yeah, right." Molly's expression suggested he was grasping at straws.

"I'll make a plan." He was very, very good at getting what he wanted. When he had a goal in mind, it took a nuclear missile strike to knock him off course. It was how he built up a chain of indie breweries and gastropubs, becoming a millionaire by the time he was thirty.

He was single-minded and ruthless and had tunnel vision. Very little was of importance to him outside his work.

Molly had once been everything he ever wanted, desired or craved. And a part of him was terrified that if he allowed his guard to fall, even a little, she would become important to him again.

Not happening, not ever again. Control. He needed to find it. And hold on to it.

"Once you find him full-time help you could move into one of the lakeside cottages if you want to."

Mack stared at her, noticing the blue stripes beneath her lovely eyes. She was tired and more than a little stressed. He knew she loved Jameson and was worried about him, but he was on the mend. The hotel might be teetering but it wasn't about to go under. And even if it was, Molly had to know that, between them, he and his brothers would, and could, inject a healthy amount of cash to keep it going.

So what was really worrying her?

And why did he care?

Mack rubbed the back of his head and considered her question. The cottages were pretty, had awesome views but weren't private. "No, I don't want to bump into any of the guests. Any other options?"

"My old house—the manager's house—is vacant at the moment."

He heard, from Jameson, that the three-bedroomed staff house had been converted into a self-catering villa years ago. Mack suspected that it hadn't, like so many other of the resort's rooms and free-standing cottages on the edge of the lake, seen many guests lately.

"Why don't you live in that house, like the hotel managers usually do?"

"It's far too big for me," Molly replied. "I asked Jameson if I could convert the rooms above the stables into an apartment and he agreed. I live there."

The stables were a stone's throw from her old house, the only two buildings on the west side of the property. The enormous parking area and a large swath of woods separated the two buildings from the other staff cottages.

The house, he recalled from visiting on those early playdates with Molly, had a wide veranda and great views of the Blue Ridge Mountains. Yeah, he'd be comfortable there.

"Your old house will work for me. I'll get the key from the front desk."

"Don't bother." Molly walked back over to her desk, her stride long and sexy, and bent over slightly to open another desk drawer. She pulled out a key and tossed it at his head. Mack, knowing she couldn't hit a barn door from two feet with a BB gun, lifted his left hand and snatched the key out of the air. He had excellent reflexes, but Molly's throws had never been much of a challenge.

That, at least, hadn't changed.

Molly rubbed her forehead with her fingertips. "If there's nothing else, will you excuse me? I'm hours behind and it's not even ten yet."

Mack nodded and slowly stood up. Unable to help himself, he walked over to where Molly stood and gently, so very gently, pushed a crazy curl behind one ear. His fingertip brushed her cheek and her skin was still baby soft but her scent was sexy, a little wicked.

"It *is* good to see you, Mol."

Molly, because she was Molly, slapped his hand away and stood back. "Too little, too late, Mack. Now go. I have work to do."

Mack lifted his hands and backed away, resisting the urge to haul her into his arms and kiss her until her knees buckled and sexy little groans emerged from deep in her throat. He still, dammit to hell and back, wanted her.

Not going to happen, Holloway, so get that thought out of your stubborn brain.

Focus on what you can control. And that was work. Talking of…

"Please schedule a meeting with senior management at two this afternoon. I want a SWOT analysis—strengths, weaknesses, opportunities and threats—"

"I have a post-grad degree in business, Holloway. I know what a SWOT analysis is, for goodness' sake!" Molly told him, looking offended.

Right. He remembered hearing she'd gotten her master's in business administration sometime back. If he didn't think she'd bite his head off, he'd congratulate her on that achievement.

"I want them to do one for their department, one for the organization as a whole, then you and I will take those, see what we're missing and work out a plan of action," Mack told her.

Molly nodded at the file on her desk. "I have already done all that."

"Bring copies of your documentation to the meeting, but I want their perspective, too," Mack stated.

Molly stared at him like he was losing his mind. "They can't get that done in—" she checked her watch, a cheap knockoff of a well-known brand "—five hours."

"I'm not looking for a perfectly printed glossy brochure, Molly," he replied, looking down at her bright and detailed folder. "I just need a list, a starting point."

"Still..."

"Two o'clock, in the conference room. I presume it's unoccupied."

"You presume right," Molly said, her tone sarcastic once again. "We haven't had a conference here for quite a while."

Why not? It didn't make any sense.

Mack placed his hand on the door and pulled it open. Looking over his shoulder, he frowned at her. "I hope you aren't going to let the past color our working relationship, Molly."

He saw the anger flash in those extraordinary eyes, the flush that tinged her cheeks pink. Man, she was beautiful...

And off-limits.

She pointed to the door and her voice, when she spoke, was shaky. "Get the hell out of my office."

Mack, recognizing the signs of her temper, thought it prudent to step into the hallway. Pulling the door shut behind him, he rested his forehead on her door and gently banged it against the thick panel. *Right, excellent attempt at making amends, friends and influencing people, Holloway.*

Not.

Three

A week later, as was her habit, Molly left her office, walked toward the rose garden and veered right onto a path designed to meander through the wild garden. Mack still hadn't found a nurse for Jameson and, instead of overseeing the resort, he was filling in as his father's nurse, with the once-fired Rylee stopping by twice a day to check vitals and dispense meds, and to be on call for emergencies. Judging by the constant barrage of text messages she'd received from Jameson, it wasn't going well and Jameson had fired his son on three occasions. Mack, as he'd told her when she stopped in to check on them yesterday, told her to keep bail money ready because blood was about to be spilled. He didn't specify whose.

Molly slipped through the gate that allowed her access onto Jameson's private property. After greeting Jameson's golden retrievers, Trouble and Nonsense, she stepped into his huge open-plan kitchen and dining room, the double-volume space dominated by exposed wooden roof beams. A few years back Jameson converted the barn with an eye to the future, creating large bedrooms with en suite bathrooms on the second floor and installing a massive dining table to accommodate his sons, daughters-in-law and all their children.

So far not one of his sons was falling in line with his plans.

Families—they were such weird entities, Molly mused. Jameson once had the perfect family, but it was ripped apart by the hand of fate. She had two brothers and a mother but she had no illusions of her importance in their lives; they neither loved nor liked her. She was, simply, their personal cash machine, a means to an end. But she still had trouble emotionally, physically and financially divorcing herself from them.

She'd never had much of a family, but she was

stronger now than when she was a child and she could, and would, tackle the world on her own. And she might have to, if Jameson banished her from Moonlight Ridge after she confessed her sins.

Molly felt her stomach knot at the thought. She'd lose her home, a job she adored, the respect of the man who'd guided, advised and loved her all of her life. Was her self-respect, being able to move forward with a clear conscience, worth the price she'd have to pay?

Molly shoved her hands into her hair and tugged, feeling herself whirling away on a tornado of self-doubt. Was losing Jameson too high a price to pay? *Yes.*

If she remained silent, could she live with herself? *No.*

She was stuck between the devil and the deep blue sea. And she was drowning.

But this wasn't the right time to confess as his neurosurgeon warned them that Jameson couldn't be subjected to any stress, that he had to be, for a few months at least, shielded from any anxiety-causing issues. The knowledge that she'd stolen from him would send his blood pressure skyrocketing, risking an actual brain aneurysm this time.

Molly placed her hands on the cool wood of the dining table and stared at the golden surface. She couldn't confess and she couldn't talk to anyone about her it-keeps-me-awake-at-night worries about the resort.

So what could she do?

Molly straightened her shoulders. She could do her job and manage the resort to the best of her ability. So far working with Mack had been tolerable, mostly because she could, mostly, pretend he wasn't there. He was spending all his time with Jameson and, she presumed, keeping tabs on his own business empire. He'd call every morning at nine o'clock sharp and ask if there were any problems.

The only problem was his deep, sexy voice, the one that fueled her X-rated dreams. Mack, naked, his expression intense, saying her name as he—

"Molly?"

Molly stood up so fast her head swam and she grabbed the back of the nearest chair to keep her balance. Within seconds Mack's strong hands were holding her biceps, steadying her. Then she made the mistake of breathing deeply and she inhaled his scent, immediately transported back to summer nights, hot and muggy, skinny-dipping in the pond before climbing up into the treehouse to lie on the rickety deck beneath the stars to intimately explore, with inexperienced hands, the wonder of each other's bodies.

Molly lifted her eyes to his and his fingertips dug into her bare skin as he pulled her closer. She wanted to step back, thought she should, but her feet wouldn't obey her brain's sugges-tion. Mack's hands slid down her arms to link his fingers in his and she watched, fascinated, as his mouth dropped to hers. He took his time to reach her mouth and, impatient, Molly couldn't wait so she stood on her tiptoes to taste him. Her eyes closed as his lips met hers and she sighed, ignoring the thought that this felt right, that she was finally home.

Mack placed a hand on her lower back to pull her closer to him, close enough for her to feel the hard, very hard, ridge of his erection push-ing into her stomach, close enough to feel the shudder that ran through him.

They shouldn't be doing this, but his mouth on

hers was the sweetest honey, the tartest spice. Sexy and demanding and amazing.

Entranced, Molly wound her arms around Mack's neck, her fingers pushing into his silky hair. Holding her palm against his head, she kept his mouth on hers, needing him to take the kiss deeper, harder. Mack heard her silent plea and slid his tongue into her mouth, finding hers and leading it into a hot, desperate dance. Time and memories faded and she was seventeen again, lost in his touch, happy to follow where he led.

Teeth scraped, tongues dueled and hands raced as they fell into the moment, the deliciousness of the forbidden. Mack rediscovered the shape of her butt and she realized that his chest was broad, muscular, and his shoulders wide. Mack pushed his thigh between her legs and Molly just managed to resist rubbing herself against him. But she couldn't resist pulling his shirt from his cargo shorts, discovering the smooth skin of his back, feeling the hard muscles of his ladderlike stomach.

They had to stop this before they couldn't…

But not yet, not just yet. She wanted more, his

fingers—or his mouth—on her nipples, between her legs…

Molly ran her hand over his fly, heard his groan as he pushed his erection into her palm, his mouth on her neck. She moved her thumb to rub his tip but encountered…

Nothing. Fresh air.

Molly blinked, shook her head and realized that Mack had stepped away from her, hurriedly yanking his blue button-down shirt over his shorts. Not knowing where she was or, frankly, *who* she was, Molly hauled in some air and tried to get her brain to fire up. As her eyes started to focus, she raised her eyebrows at Mack, who nodded to the kitchen door.

"Company," he mouthed.

Blushing, then grimacing, Molly turned to look at the half-open stable door. Molly instantly recognized that dark head and the tiny frame. Giada worked for Jameson as a housekeeper at Moonlight Ridge years ago, and Molly hadn't seen the tiny lady for far too long.

Her embarrassment forgotten, Molly hurried across the kitchen and opened the bottom half of the stable door and pulled Giada into a hug.

After they separated, Molly kept hold of her hands. "Oh, it's so, so good to see you."

Giada raised her hand to hold Molly's face. "*Cara mia*, you are so beautiful. And all grown up!"

"When did you get back to town?" Molly demanded, pulling her into the kitchen. "Are you still living with your sister in Florida?"

Grief skittered through Giada's eyes. "She died a few months ago."

"I'm so sorry," Molly murmured. Hoping that her face was no longer bloodred, she gestured to Mack. "Obviously, you remember Mack?"

Mack bent down, and down, to kiss both of Giada's cheeks. "It's so good to see you, Giada."

"Mack." Giada ran her hands up and down his well-muscled arms. "My, my, you have grown into a beautiful man."

Mack's smile was wide and genuine and Molly's traitorous heart flipped over. And over again. "Not as beautiful as you, gorgeous. As Molly said, it's wonderful to see you."

Giada's eyes, filled with amusement, darted from his face to hers and back again. "You are being too kind. From what I saw, you two are probably cursing me to hell and back for inter-rupting."

Molly winced. Giada never did beat around the bush when she could plow through it.

Mack slid his hands into his pockets. "I presume you are here to see Jameson?"

Right, judging by his inscrutable expression, no one would suspect that he'd just had his hand up and under her shirt. She had no doubt that someone half-blind could see that she'd been thoroughly kissed. Though *kissed* was too tame a word for what they'd done...

Inhaled each other might be a better description.

"I am. Is he up to visitors?" Giada asked.

Mack nodded. "He's in his sitting room, down the hallway and on your left. I'm sure he'd be very glad to see you," Mack stated. "We'll join you in a few minutes."

They both watched her walk away and when Molly was sure she was out of earshot, she forced herself to look at Mack. Feeling a little shaky, she pulled out a chair from the dining table and sank down onto its seat, dropping her head.

Holy, holy crap.

Molly heard Mack moving toward her and

watched as he rested his hip against the table, not far from her head. He was too close and it gave her ideas...

Bad ideas...like reaching for his fly and picking up where they'd left off.

God.

Help.

Her.

"That shouldn't have happened."

Molly lifted her head to look up, stopping at his impassive expression. His eyes were shuttered and he looked like he was about to launch into a discussion about cash flows and profit margins. "Thank you, Captain Obvious," Molly muttered.

"In case you are wondering whether we are going to pick up where we left off, that's not going to happen," Mack said, his voice cool but sharp. "I'm only here for a short time and I'm not looking for a relationship. I don't do relationships. Hell, I barely do flings."

Her mouth fell open, not quite able to believe the words he was spouting, that he could be so damn arrogant to assume that, just because he was here again, she wanted to dive back into his arms and bed.

She'd just kissed him, not proposed marriage or offered to have his babies…

The *moron*.

Molly pushed her chair back and stood, all traces of her embarrassment gone and replaced by cold anger. She met his eyes and when his widened, she knew that he'd clocked her temper. "Are you freaking kidding me? Why would you assume that?"

"Uh—"

Molly slapped her hand on his hard pec and pushed him, annoyed that she couldn't budge him. "How incredibly arrogant of you to think that, just because you are back in my life, I'd welcome you back into my bed. I may have missed you, but you left me without a word. I haven't had a proper conversation with you in years and I'm solidly, completely, massively pissed at you! You acted like a jerk and I'd rather sleep with a snake!"

"Then why did you kiss me like I was your last hit of oxygen?" Mack demanded.

Calm down, Molly, and do not let him see how rattled you truly are.

"C'mon, Mack, we've been combustible since the first time we made out. We may have changed but that hasn't," Molly said, trying to lighten her tone. "It was just a kiss, no big deal."

"It feels like it's a big deal," Mack countered.

Arrgh, why was he pushing this? "I'll admit you broke my teenage heart but I'm very over you, Holloway."

Mack scrubbed his hands over his face and when he dropped them, Molly saw remorse within those dark depths. Too little, too late.

Knowing he was about to apologize and not wanting to hear it, she lifted her hand to speak. "Let me just say this, Mack, and then, hopefully, we can move on. I missed my boyfriend, but God, I *mourned* my best friend. And you will never, ever get the chance to hurt me like that again."

Squaring her shoulders, she pushed away the tang of acidic emotions and stepped into the hallway. She'd visit with Jameson and Giada and then she'd head back to her office. It was getting late but she had work to do, reports to read, staff schedules to post, requisitions to authorize…

A business to save.

Mack watched Molly's lovely figure walk away and pushed a frustrated hand through his hair. He was all about control, it was his guiding principle, a core tenet of his life. As an adult, and intellectually, he knew his mom's death was not his fault—how could it be?—but that hadn't stopped his biological dad from blaming him and taking his anger out on his young son.

His dad's uncontrollable temper scared him and he loved Jameson's steadiness and lack of volatility and tried to emulate his nonblood father. The one time he lost complete control had disastrous consequences, so these days he always thought twice—thrice—and acted once. He never ever allowed emotion to guide him and what he wanted was always tempered with thoughts about what he needed and whether he could live with all the possible consequences of his actions.

Since leaving Asheville he'd been careful, thoughtful, conservative...

But Molly Haskell could blow him out of the water. She still smelled the same, looked, in many ways, the same, but there was a strength to her now that intrigued him, a confidence that hadn't been there fifteen years ago. And that, he supposed, made sense. She'd grown up.

And, Mack thought, remembering her perfect

breast under his hand, the curve of her stupendous butt, she'd grown up damn fine.

Stop it, Holloway, for crap's sake. She's just another gorgeous woman. He'd met, and bedded, quite a few since he was eighteen. But none of his past lovers had Molly's ability to crawl under his skin, upend his life and muddle his brain.

Molly, damn her, wasn't someone he could easily dismiss.

So far life in Asheville was anything but boring. In between trying not to throttle his irascible and demanding father, Mack kept tabs on what was happening with his chain of breweries and gastropubs and, when he had a spare moment, tried to get a handle on what was happening with the resort. But uncharacteristically, he was often distracted by the memories of how Molly loved him so long ago. His lips on hers, her hand on his shaft…

The memory of her pain and disappointment slapped at him, hard and fast. If they were going to work together, Mack reluctantly conceded, they were going to have to address the past. Properly. Their brief conversation last week had barely scratched the surface.

And...

He'd rather have a hot ember rammed into his eye.

But he'd hurt her and he regretted that. Mack wondered what she would say if he told her that he spent many nights thinking of her, missing her with every atom of his being. Would she be surprised to hear that, in the weeks and months after leaving, he'd often woken with a wet-from-tears pillowcase, feeling like a bowling ball was residing in his stomach? That he, on a hundred occasions, maybe more, picked up his phone to call her, just to hear her voice?

He was pretty sure that she had no idea that when he'd left, he cut out his own heart, too.

But he hadn't been able to stay. The guilt had been intense, his relationships with his brothers were annihilated and Mack couldn't fathom how Jameson could love him after what he did. In losing control, he'd failed his father and his brothers.

After he left Asheville, school slid into work and he immersed himself in his business, establishing brewery after brewery, adding gastropubs to the mix. He had a fancy loft apartment, a cabin in Whistler, cars and toys and a crapload of cash in the bank, numerous women he could call on if he needed company…

He worked. Played a little. Worked out. Worked and worked out some more.

Existed.

But kissing Molly was the most alive he'd felt in years. When she stepped into his arms and her mouth touched his, she became the watering can and he the starved-for-nutrients plant. Excitement and need coursed through him and if Giada hadn't banged on the door, he knew their kiss would've moved from hot to nuclear.

Mack held his palm parallel to the ground and shook his head when he saw the slight tremor in his fingers. She made him feel like this: shaky, weird, out of control.

That wasn't acceptable.

Right, he needed to nip this in the bud. He'd have a decent discussion with her, apologize for leaving her and ask whether they could put the past behind them. Once she accepted his apology—Molly had never been one to hold grudges—they could move on. He'd keep his interactions with her as brief and as professional as possible.

It would be fine. It *had* to be fine. He would

not let Molly—and his being back home—make him lose sight of what was important.

And that was keeping control. Keeping it together. He was determined to leave here with his heart intact, his world unchanged.

Sorted, Mack thought as he walked down the hallway to join Giada and Molly in Jameson's downstairs sitting room.

It annoyed Jameson that he couldn't leap to his feet when Giada walked into his small sitting room off his large, ground-floor master suite. He was an old-fashioned Southern man and it galled him that he neither had the energy nor the strength to leap to his feet like he always did.

Energy was something still in short supply and he was sick of feeling like crap. Jameson ran his hand over his stubbled jaw and, briefly, wished he'd shaved. But he wouldn't let Mack help him and he still tired easily. But if he was better at accepting assistance and if he had a little more patience, he'd look a lot better than he currently did.

That wasn't a problem his ex-housekeeper had.

She barely looked any older than she did when she worked for him twenty years ago. Her hair was still thick and wavy and he liked the threads of gray breaking up all that rich brown. Her blue eyes were as direct as ever and Jameson shifted in his chair, thinking that she could look right into his soul. Her body was, maybe, a little curvier, and there were fine lines at the corners of her take-no-bull eyes. For a woman in her late fifties, she was damn sexy.

He felt like day-old roadkill.

Jameson inhaled her perfume as she bent down to kiss his cheek, surprised at the hint of action in his pants. Okay, so his attraction to Giada hadn't changed. He'd been into her a long time ago but circumstances—her working for him and the fact that he had his hands full running Moonlight Ridge and raising three boys—conspired against his making a move.

"Jameson—" Giada kept her hands on his shoulders and shook her head "—you look like hell."

Great. Exactly what he needed to hear. "Giada. You're the very last person I expected today."

Giada sat down in the chair opposite him and lifted her shoulders in a languid, oh-so-Italian shrug. "I came back to Asheville, heard that you have been ill and thought I'd check up on you."

Her eyes moved to the ashtray sitting on the side table next to his easy chair, and a deep frown pulled her dark, thin eyebrows together. The smoke from his cigar drifted toward the roof.

"Mannaggia a te!" Giada muttered. He didn't speak Italian but he recognized curse words when they were directed at him.

Before he could respond, she surged to her feet, picked up the cigar and crushed its tip, mangling it into a mess.

"Hey, those are expensive!"

"You've had brain surgery! Surely, your doctor told you to stop smoking?" Giada demanded, her hands on those luscious hips. She was short, the top of her head barely hit his shoulder, but she was feisty. And fierce.

He was saved from having to find an excuse, not that he had or needed one—if he wanted to smoke he damn well could!—by Molly stepping into the room. Jameson accepted her kiss and when she stepped back, noticed she was looking tired. And stressed.

He had no doubt that she and Mack had exchanged words.

M&M, he used to call them, his two peas in a pod. His oldest son and the daughter of his heart.

Watching her heart break after Mack left had been pure torture, but apart from putting her to work to keep her busy and her mind off Mack, he hadn't interfered.

Raising three boys had never been a walk in the park but those few months directly after the accident had been a shit show. In hindsight, he knew that most of his energies had been directed toward Travis, spending hours and hours with him at the hospital. He'd been there for his injured son, but he'd failed to realize his two other sons were as psychologically damaged as Travis was physically hurt.

Grey retreated mentally and emotionally and Mack had dealt with his guilt and pain by running. There were still walls between him and his boys—lower than they'd been before—but still there. Jameson wanted them gone. And he wanted his sons to be brothers again, as tight as they were when they were kids. And if it took a freaking brain aneurysm to get his boys back and talking to each other, then so be it.

Failing that, he'd just bash their heads together...

Molly rubbed her thumb over his frown lines. "You're not supposed to be worrying, Jameson."

Jameson captured her hand and pressed a kiss onto her fingers. "Don't fuss, Mol."

"It's what I do best," Molly told him, sitting down next to him on the sofa.

"Did you see Mack?" Jameson asked her.

Jameson heard a snort of laughter from Giada and lifted his eyebrows, silently asking what she found amusing. Giada just grinned and shrugged.

"Yep." He frowned at her terse answer since Molly was normally a talker. Hopefully, while they worked together, something would spark between them again. *Two birds, one stone*, Jameson thought.

M&M were destined to be together and when they pulled their heads out of their butts, they'd catch that clue.

Jameson, conscious that he hadn't paid his guest any attention—and he wanted to—turned to Giada. "I heard from someone that you went to nursing school and that you graduated." He'd once offered to pay for her education but Giada, like Molly—God save him from stubborn women!—refused his offer. They'd both worked part-time jobs to put themselves through school and he admired their effort but it had been so damn unnecessary.

Really, life would be so much easier for all involved if people just did as he commanded!

Giada nodded. "I moved to Florida to attend school and to be closer to my sister. After I graduated, I worked in the ER for more than ten years. A year ago I took a sabbatical to nurse my sister through terminal cancer. I'm not sure what's next or where I want to be."

Jameson offered his condolences before asking his next question. "Are you thinking about moving back to Asheville, finding work here?" He really hoped so; he would like to see her again. When he was well, and back to full strength, he might even ask her out to dinner, to the theater. And then into his bed...

He really, *really* wanted her in his bed.

Giada's eyes twinkled, as if she knew where his thoughts had veered to. She'd always had the ability to do that, to look below the surface and see what he was thinking. He wasn't sure if he liked it.

Giada crossed her legs, tanned and smooth. She wore wedge sandals and her toes were painted bright orange. He had a thing for pretty feet, lovely legs and gorgeous Italian women…

"My sister left me quite a lot of money," Giada replied, "but I'm easily bored so I might look for some work soon. But not in the trauma ward. That's a little too intense for me. I need to find something to do. I get into trouble when I'm not busy."

That, he could believe. Luckily, there was lots to do in Asheville, he wanted to tell her. She'd just walked back into his life; he didn't want her walking out again so soon.

"What about a job looking after a cranky, stubborn, annoying survivor of a brain episode?"

Jameson whipped his head toward the door to where Mack stood, his legs and arms crossed, leaning into the door frame. Jameson lifted his hand to make a slashing movement against his throat, scowling madly.

He did not want, or need, the lovely Giada nursing him, fussing over him. No, thank you; a man had his pride. And he had more than most.

"That's a really good idea," Molly said, her eyes brightening.

No, it wasn't. It really damn wasn't!

"She's qualified, she's tough and, best of all,

you don't scare her." Molly looked at Giada, who was looking as shocked as he felt. "What do you think, Giada? Jameson is spectacularly grouchy and none of his nurses stick."

"You are exaggerating and I can manage just fine on my own," Jameson muttered, sending Giada a pleading look. *Please say no; please don't consider this idea.* He couldn't bear it.

But he also didn't want her to leave the area. God knew when he'd see her again.

"You need a nurse," Mack told him, his voice brooking no argument. Jameson heard the authority in his voice and realized that his son was a man. And a man who took no crap.

Well, he was a man, too, and he'd never taken any crap. He started to stand up, realized that he couldn't and silently, but violently, repeated a long, vulgar string of curses.

He was weak, dammit. And maybe he could do with a little help.

Mack stepped into the room, his eyes on Giada. "We really do need someone to help him, Giada. We're driving each other insane. The salary is generous and, because we know how annoying he can be—" Mack's lips quirking took the sting out of that comment "—we'll make sure you have plenty of free time."

Giada looked like she was seriously considering Mack's offer. Oh, God, help him.

But God wasn't on his side because Giada tipped her head to the side and pursed her lips. "Would I stay here?"

Mack nodded. "Pops converted our bedrooms into three guest suites, one with an en suite bathroom, and the other two bedrooms share a bathroom. The biggest guest suite has a sitting area and a small desk and is ready for immediate occupation. Jameson's study is right next door and he has a huge collection of books if you are a reader. The resort's kitchen will provide you food. Housekeeping takes care of the house. You just have to deal with Mr. Grumpy."

Funny. *Not.*

Jameson held his breath, not wanting her to agree, but because he really wanted to see her again, hoped she would.

"He won't be allowed to smoke," Giana warned them.

"Fine with me." Mack swiftly replied.

"And me," Molly chirped.

Traitors. "Not fine with me," he growled.

"I want to talk to his doctors and get proper instructions on his care," Giada insisted, her pretty lips pursed.

"I'll make that happen," Mack told her.

"I am sitting right here," Jameson told them, raising his voice. "Do I not get a say in all of this?"

Three sets of inquiring eyes rested on his face. Mack lifted his hands. "Sure, go ahead, Pops."

"I'm not comfortable with this. I'd prefer to have a stranger nursing me."

"Then you shouldn't have fired the past three intensely professional nurses the agency sent you," Mack told him.

"And Giada doesn't take any crap," Molly said. She darted a look at Mack. "Do you remember her losing her temper when she found us in her linen cupboard?"

"That was because you ate chocolate in that cupboard and put your sticky fingers on my fresh white towels," Giada shot back.

Molly grimaced. "I forgot that part."

Giada's grin was a little smug. "I didn't." Her eyes slammed into Jameson's and within them, he saw the silent challenge...

Can you handle me, Holloway?

At full strength, with one hand behind his back. And any way she wanted him to. Right now? He wasn't so sure...

If she came to work for him, they'd fight but at least he wouldn't be bored. The nurses he'd banished had either been too insipid or too bossy but Giada, at least, was interesting. She wouldn't take his crap.

And he wouldn't take hers.

Yeah, he wouldn't be bored.

"Is that a yes?" Giada asked, her voice soft.

"Suppose so," Jameson replied, less than graciously. He looked down at his mangled cigar and grimaced. "Just don't mess with my cigars."

Giada sent him an evil smile. "I won't need to because, from this moment on, you are not going to be smoking anymore."

Right, gloves on. She would need to learn that she couldn't push him around. "Not happening."

Giada stood up, placed her hands on her hips and glared at him. "Want to bet?"

"You wouldn't dare!"

"Watch me!"

As they squared off, neither of them noticed Molly and Mack tiptoeing out of the room.

Four

"How long do you think it'll take for blood to spill?" Mack asked her, his voice low as his broad hand on her back guided her through the wrought iron gate and onto the path that would take them, if they went south, to the main lodge, and north, to their respective houses.

Annoyed that his light touch could send tingles along her skin, Molly stepped away from him and pushed her hand into her hair, holding a bunch of curls off her face. "An hour, two if we are lucky."

"Well, my money is on Giada. That lady is tough."

Molly nodded, feeling awkward. What did one

say to a man whom she'd once loved but who was now little more than a stranger? Someone she'd barely spoken to for the past week, despite kissing him like he was her last hit of oxygen? Someone she was still attracted to, a man who still managed to light a fire in her belly, who made her tingle down…well, everywhere. Her body had front-row seats to her heartbreak; how could it betray her like this?

But maybe she was also overreacting. It had been a tough few weeks, she was overwhelmed by work and terrified that Moonlight Ridge would fall apart under her watch. She'd been desperately worried about Jameson, and her family was bugging her for cash again.

Kissing Mack was a way to step out, to avoid reality. And to remind her that she was a normal woman with normal needs. Needs she'd been neglecting for a long, long time. Man, this was all so complicated, and she didn't have time or the energy for complicated.

Molly sighed, wishing he'd just go and send one of his brothers to deal with Moonlight Ridge. Travis and Grey she could handle. Mack? Not so much.

Or at all.

Molly gestured to the path. "It's been a long day. I'm going to go."

Mack placed his hands into the back pockets of his cargo shorts, causing his blue button-down shirt to pull across his broad chest and to bunch around his impressive biceps. Molly resisted the urge to fan her face. "I'll walk with you for a while and stretch my legs. Then I'll go back and finalize the arrangements with Giada. Hopefully, she'll be able to start immediately because I'm a shocking nurse."

"And Jameson is a shocking patient," Molly murmured before shaking her head. "You don't need to walk with me, Mack."

Mack scrubbed the back of his neck. "It'll give us a chance to clear the air, Molly, and I think that's what we need to do, especially since we are going to be working closely together for the next few weeks. We should've done this days ago, but taking care of my dad was more time-consuming than I'd thought."

Molly wrinkled her nose. She was hot, tired and out of sorts and she wasn't up for a discussion about the past. And Mack, she was sure, was only broaching this subject because it was expedient for him to do so. To oversee Moonlight Ridge, he needed her cooperation. Mack had always been single-minded and stubborn and Molly had no doubt he was ruthless, as well—few men achieved his level of success without that trait—and he'd do what was necessary to get the result he wanted. And if that included smoothing the ruffled feathers of his irritable ex-girlfriend, that was what he'd do.

She had no intention of making life easy for him.

Stepping away from him, Molly crossed her arms and tapped her foot. "A hot kiss and a quick chat after fifteen years won't change the past, Mack. Are you really that arrogant to think that I would be so grateful that you are back, so happy to be in your arms again, that I would fall into line like a good little soldier?"

She saw surprise flash in his eyes and knew he had been thinking just that. *Arrogant much, Holloway?*

"We were kids, Molly. It was a long time ago," Mack said, his tone reflecting a hint of annoyance. "We can move on, surely?"

He wanted her to, that much was obvious. And under that inscrutable face, she caught hints of his frustration. It was in the tiny tick in the muscle running down his jaw, in the tightening of the fine lines next to his eyes. In the flattening of his lips. Oh, most people wouldn't pick up the subtle changes in his expression but she could look beneath the surface better than most. After all, his had always been her favorite face.

"As I said, I'm not mad because you broke up with me, Mack," Molly told him, keeping her voice level. Losing her temper would only make her look childish.

"We would be having a completely different conversation if you actually *told* me you were leaving, if you only left after an explanation and a goodbye. But you didn't call and when you came back here, you avoided me. Every single time. Not once in fifteen years did you try to talk to me, to check up on me, or attempt to reboot our friendship.

"You've been back many times and on any one of those occasions you could've tracked me down, had a conversation, made a goddamn effort! Not because we once loved each other but because we were best *friends*, Mack. Friends don't treat each other like that," Molly added.

Mack dropped his head to stare at the stone path, his mouth pulled into grim lines. "For what it's worth, I am sorry, Curls. I never meant to hurt you and I hope you can forgive me."

Her heart did a triple beat of his old nickname for her, but one she hadn't heard for a decade and a half. But she couldn't let that distract her...

She finally had the proper apology she'd been waiting for. She'd been waiting for this moment for fifteen years but now that it was here, she didn't know what to do with it, how to handle him, what to say, what to do next. All she knew was that she was exhausted and that she didn't want to argue anymore.

"Thank you and your apology is accepted." Molly managed a small smile. Ha, look at her, adulting here!

"I'm going to go," Molly added when he failed to break the uncomfortable silence between them.

"Maybe we should talk about what happened in Jameson's kitchen," Mack stated, jamming his hands into the pockets of his shorts.

Oh, God, she didn't want to talk about the past but neither did she want to discuss her insane reaction to his mouth and hands and his strong, sexy body. "It was a *kiss*, Holloway. Don't get excited." Molly smiled to take the sting out of her words. "You're a good-looking guy and I got caught up in the moment. It won't happen again."

The tiniest hint of a smile turned his stern face a degree warmer. "Oh, I think it will."

"You should talk to someone about your delusions, Holloway." Molly forced herself to hold his intense gaze, to keep smiling. She would rather be pulled through a field covered in barbed wire than give Mack an inch. "It was momentary madness. Don't read more into it than that."

"The chemistry between us is still running hot."

Thanks for pointing that out, Einstein. "We kissed. It was a *mistake*. Let's forget about it and move on."

"Easy to say, less easy to do."

"Well, we can damn well try," Molly said, cursing the agitation in her voice. "Mack, I'm exhausted. It's been a long, long day and all I want is a huge glass of wine. As for us working together, I will be professional but that's it. There will be no personal conversations and no physical contact. Are we clear?"

Mack opened his mouth to argue—she recognized his need to always have the last word—but instead of speaking, he shook his head.

Thirty seconds passed before he spoke again. "We can try. I'm not sure how successful we'll be."

He thought she was just going to fall back into his arms, oh so grateful to be with him again. Was he completely nuts? Okay, their kiss had caught her off guard, but it was a mistake, and she couldn't allow herself to repeat past missteps. Mack hurt her; she'd never allow him to do that again. As for their attraction, well, he was a good-looking guy and it had been a long time since she'd had any bedroom-based fun.

And if she was overdue for some naked fun, she could head into town, find a bar and pick someone up. She'd never had a one-night stand but how hard could it be?

What she wouldn't do was let Mack Holloway upend her world. Once bitten, twice shy, blah, blah...

Molly looked up into Mack's face and sighed. If only he wasn't so damn sexy. High cheekbones, that square-ish jaw and pointed chin, his straight nose. That hot, sexy mouth and the rough stubble on his cheeks. He was such a *man*...

But he wasn't the man for her.

"Have a good evening, Mack. I'll see you in the morning," Molly told him, pushing past him to walk up the path toward her apartment above the stable. A part of her was done, ready to collapse into a heap; another part of her wanted to grab her leotard and tights and head into Asheville to work out her frustration in a hip-hop class. It wasn't ballet but it was still moving her body in time to the music. It counted.

She might dance first, collapse later.

All she knew for sure was that she had to put some distance, physical and emotional, between her and Holloway.

The next day Mack, on his way to Jameson's office on the third floor of the inn, caught movement out of the corner of his eye as he passed Molly's office. Stopping, he looked through the half-open office door and frowned when he saw a woman looming over Molly's desk, her index finger under Molly's nose.

Beth, Moonlight Ridge's bookkeeper. He'd met her at last week's senior management meeting. And he hadn't been impressed.

Mack cleared his throat and two heads whipped

around to look at him. Frustration and annoyance skittered across Beth's face while Molly just looked relieved...

What the hell was going on here?

Mack leaned his shoulder into the door frame, crossed his foot over his ankle and lifted his eyebrows. "Am I interrupting something?"

Judging by their expressions, he very obviously was. Molly was frowning and her lovely eyes—light green today—reflected her anxiety. And her annoyance.

And the fact that this woman—tall, slim, generically beautiful—could make her feel like that annoyed *him*.

"Is there a problem here?" Mack demanded, keeping his voice even but making sure Beth heard the authority in it.

He'd be a fool not to see the warning glance Beth threw Molly's way. Oh yeah, she was stirring a bubbling pot with a long-handled spoon.

Beth flashed him a smile that was meant to impress, or distract, him. It did neither. "Good morning, Mack. Molly and I were just chatting about the family."

"And what family would that be?" Mack asked.

Beth fiddled with a button on her too-tight

shirt, a movement that was supposed to draw his eye to her impressive cleavage. Not wanting to play her game, he kept his eyes on her face and noticed her tiny pout.

"Why, the Haskells of course," Beth replied, her too-high voice still cheerful but her eyes flat and wary.

"Beth and Grant have been together for the past six months, Mack," Molly reluctantly explained.

Ah.

Beth touched the messy bun on the back of her head, the movement lifting her chest, and breasts, up. Mack did an internal eye roll. *Okay, I get it, you've got great tits.*

Strike one.

As Mack walked into the room, his eyes moved on to Molly and he spent a minute taking her in. She wore a white sleeveless top that showed off her toned arms, and through the silky material, he could see the outline of a lacy bra. A pendant, a purple stone tipped with silver on a long chain, was wound twice around her neck, and her crazy curls were pulled back from her face by a multicolored scarf. Her makeup, unlike Beth's, was light and fresh and he could see the freckles under a light layer of foundation. Her eyelashes were long and coated with black mascara, making her eyes seems lighter and brighter.

God, she was gorgeous. And, despite the way they left things last night, he still wanted her.

Mack pulled his attention back to what had initially caught his attention—Beth leaning over Molly's desk, her finger in his ex's face. Nobody treated Molly like that and he was surprised she put up with it. Molly was, after all, Beth's boss.

"You weren't having a friendly, let's-catch-up chat," Mack stated. He locked eyes with Beth and studied her, keeping his expression flat and cold.

She brazenly held his eyes for ten seconds, then twenty. At twenty-five, she started to waver and by thirty her eyes had dropped to look at the floor.

"You were looming over her desk and your finger was in Molly's face—"

"We were discussing a family matter—" Beth interrupted him. As a child, before he came to live with Jameson, he could never ever finish a sentence without his biological father overriding or deriding him. As a result, he loathed being interrupted.

Strike two.

"Mack, just leave it alone," Molly jumped in and he heard the I-can-deal-with-this in her voice.

He ignored her and kept his eyes on Beth. "Molly is your boss. Personal discussions can take place outside of work. And if I ever see you looming over her and jamming your finger in her face again, you will be dismissed, instantly."

Beth's expression turned ugly. "You can't do that."

"Mack!"

Mack ignored Molly and sent Beth a cold, hard smile. "Do you want to test me on that?"

Beth opened her mouth to blast him, thought better of it—clever girl—and sent Molly a vicious, I'll-see-you-in-hell look. Picking up a folder from her desk, she slapped it against her thigh, released a frustrated huff and barreled toward the door. Mack just managed to move out of the way; if he hadn't, her shoulder would've bumped his arm as she passed by.

Good thing she didn't or else her ass would be toast.

Mack turned to watch her storm down the hallway, a little uneasy. Yeah, he instinctively didn't like her. He was quite sure the feeling was mutual and didn't give a damn.

Turning his attention back to Molly, he looked across the room to find her glaring at him. He lifted his hands in a what-did-I-do gesture. "What?"

Molly put her hands on her desk, shoved her chair back and shot to her feet. "That was a private conversation and you had no right to interfere!"

Mack jammed his hands into the pockets of his chino pants. "That wasn't a conversation. She was threatening you."

"She was not threatening me!" Molly retorted, so quickly that he knew she was lying. "And, even if she was, I'm a big girl. I can fight my own battles. I don't need you to defend me anymore, Mack."

He'd been her protector as a kid, standing between her and her bigger, older, meaner brothers. She'd been an easy target for those two bullies until he, and his brothers, made it clear Molly was off-limits.

Back then the three Holloway brothers had been a force to be reckoned with.

The day they heard Grant and Vincent would be leaving the resort, they cheered loudly, happy to be rid of them. Then they realized that Molly would be leaving, too. Mack begged Jameson to allow Molly to move in with them; they needed a sister, he'd pleaded.

He hadn't spoken to Jameson for two days when he told them that Molly had to leave with her family.

Mack looked into her flashing eyes and felt the stirring in his pants. Yeah, it had been a long, long time since he thought of Molly Haskell in a sisterly way.

Mack dropped into the chair on the other side of her desk and placed his elbows on the arms and made a triangle with his index fingers and thumbs. Something was going on with her and Beth and he wanted to know the source of their quarrel. Why? He had no damn idea.

"What did she say to you?" Mack asked.

"None of your damn business," Molly said, sinking down into her chair again and pushing her fingers into her curls, dislodging her scarf. She cursed, pulled it off her head and tossed it onto the desk and her beautiful corkscrew curls fell over her face. He remembered her curls brushing his chest as her mouth trailed across his skin, brushing his stomach...

He hardened instantly and Mack silently cursed. *Display a little control, Holloway, for the love of God!*

Molly lifted her head, straightened her keyboard and mouse pad before turning to look at him again, her eyes shuttered and her expression blank. "Was there something you wanted from me or did you just step into my office to annoy me?"

Mack sighed and dropped his hands. She had that "go away" look on her face that he remembered so well. He knew that if he pushed her now, she'd close down and clam up and she'd never trust him with the truth.

Molly had her own fair share of stubborn.

Mack pulled his brain back to business, to the reason he was on the property where he grew up.

"In between looking after my dad, I spent time going through paperwork in his home office. He keeps a lot of the accounting records there," Mack told her, still trying to pinpoint the source of his unease. Something was off with what he'd seen and he couldn't put his finger on why he felt uncomfortable.

Molly reached for the phone and paused, her hand on the receiver. "I need coffee. Do you want some?"

Mack nodded. "Sure. Thanks."

Molly placed the order with the kitchen and sat back in her chair, looking professional and polite. He doubted either would last; there was too much passion between them.

But they could try because finding themselves tangled up in each other again would be a complication neither of them needed. He certainly didn't. When he left again, he wanted no regrets.

"I have a few questions for you…"

"Okay, I'll answer what I can."

Mack thought about the disorganized and inefficient mound of papers he'd recently plowed through. "Why the hell aren't the books on a computer-based system?"

Molly threw up her hands, obviously frustrated. "Because they aren't."

That wasn't any type of answer. "Molly…" he warned and noticed her squirming in her seat. Ah, he thought he knew what this was about.

"M, I know how much you love my dad, how

much you love Moonlight Ridge. You always
have. But you *can* criticize my dad and the business decisions he's made. In fact, I'm asking you
to because if you're not totally truthful with me,
I won't get an accurate picture of what's happening."

Her shoulders slumped and relief flashed in
her eyes. "I've been trying to get Jameson to
switch over to a computer-based accounting system for years but he insists on doing things old
school. I did manage to persuade him to allow
us to create a web-based booking system but
that's as far as he would go. We've had quite a
few arguments on this subject."

He could imagine: Jameson hated change.

"Even with the department reports and your
proposal, I still don't have a clear idea what's
happening, financially, with the resort, but
something's not right."

Molly stiffened and looked away and Mack's
senses immediately went on red alert. "What
aren't you telling me, Molly?"

Molly rested her forearms on the desk and
picked up a pen and tapped it against the surface of a blank notepad, leaving tiny black dots
over the white paper. Her eyes, when they met

his, reflected her anxiety. "As I told you earlier, in my opinion, the resort is on the edge of a tipping point, Mack. My gut instinct tells me we have six months, maybe a year, before the company runs into trouble, serious trouble."

Mack's eyes widened. Damn. He'd hoped it hadn't been that bad.

"Twenty, thirty years ago, this was the ultimate hideaway for the very rich, looking for a home away from home, a place that guaranteed privacy. The guests would bring their children for six weeks, two months at a time, and this place pumped. In fact, the way Jameson tells it, it was a little like the resort in the movie *Dirty Dancing.*"

Mack grimaced. "The one you made me watch a hundred times when we were kids?"

Molly wrinkled her nose. "Twice, maybe three times. Anyway, back then the resort was crazy busy. But these days there's so much competition and we're just another luxurious resort in a market with lots of options. Costs are up, sales are down and staff is expensive."

Employing thousands himself, he knew exactly how costly staff could be. And, like Jameson, he'd believed in paying his staff well, provided they performed. But to Mack, it looked like there were too many staff members at Moonlight Ridge; the staff-to-guest ratio was insane.

"Who does the hiring and firing?"

Molly considered his question. "The individual managers put in a requisition for a staff member and once it's approved, they hire whoever they want to. Jameson believes in allowing his staff to run their department their way. Jameson handles all firing, but it's rare."

Mack gripped the bridge of his nose. He loved his dad, he did, but Jameson's strengths were in guest relations—he was a bon vivant and a genial host, a magnetic personality—but the nitty-gritty of business bored him.

A ruthless businessman he was not. In today's cutthroat business environment, you had to keep an eye on every aspect of your company and make crucial decisions—staff hires, expense approvals and asset purchases yourself—or the business could run away with you.

Molly, he believed, was the glue holding this place together.

"Tell me what you think of the senior staff," Mack commanded.

Molly grimaced, obviously not wanting to dish

dirt. When he didn't back down, she sighed her displeasure.

"Well, you met them all last week. Beth runs the accounts department—"

"She's done a piss-poor job of it," Mack muttered.

Molly nodded her agreement. "The catering and events manager, Ross Barnes, is amazing. He's been here for about five years, has a lot of experience and he's very good at his job. He works closely with Autumn Kincaid. She's our independent wedding planner.

"Milo Horton, our maintenance manager and groundskeeper, is a hard worker. Fern Matlock, our executive chef, is competent. She used to be Henri's sous-chef—"

He remembered Henri, the resort's expat chef and Travis's mentor, with fondness.

"Harry Levin runs the front desk and guest relations. Other than Jameson, there's no one better with guests than Harry." Molly continued, "And I try to keep all of them from killing each other."

"I skimmed over their ideas born out of our SWOT analysis meeting," Mack said, resting his linked fingers on his stomach. "Some were interesting, some were pie in the sky."

A knock pulled her attention off Mack. A young waiter opened the door and strode in, holding a tray laden with an expensive coffee jug and china cups and saucers. The tray he carried was silver and was part of the silver collection—along with the art and antiques collection—Jameson inherited from the previous owner, Tip O'Sullivan. Jameson had been his manager at the time and Tip, who'd never married and was childless, thought the world of Jameson.

The waiter placed the tray on Molly's desk. "Thanks, Larry."

Mack took the cup Molly handed him and rested his ankle on his opposite knee. "As I expected, yours was the most intricate, detailed and sensible plan."

"It's the proposal I'd already compiled, in preparation for my meeting with Jameson," Molly told him, wrapping her hands around her china cup.

She was good at business and he felt a spurt of pride at her prowess. "If I gave you carte blanche to do three things, what would they be?" Mack asked.

Molly didn't hesitate. "Update and renovate the rooms. Update the menu. Instigate a massive marketing drive to look for segments of the market we might've missed. We need younger, richer people to visit Moonlight Ridge, Mack. We can't rely on our old guests to keep this place running."

He agreed.

"But I'd also like to add that we need to attract upmarket weddings and conferences. Those are our best moneymakers," Molly continued, passion in her eyes. He wished she was looking at him with the same passion, but her focus was solely on Moonlight Ridge and how to restore it to its former glory.

And if there was anyone who could do it, Molly could. She was knowledgeable and dedicated, committed and smart, and Jameson was damn lucky to have kept her for this long.

"As you saw in my proposal, I have detailed budgets for each suggestion. I have ten more ideas and ten more budgets," Molly said, sounding deadly serious.

Of course she did. "Would you like to come work for me?" Mack asked, only half joking.

"We'd spend all our time arguing or—" Molly snapped her teeth together and blushed. Mack grinned, knowing what she was about to say.

"We'd either argue or get naked," Mack told her. He smiled before speaking again. "I have little appetite for the first and a great deal for the second."

He'd always told her the truth and had no intention of changing that now. "Full disclosure, M, I want to sleep with you again."

Molly's eyes, when they met his, were cool and her expression distant. "Not going to happen, Holloway."

Mack sipped his coffee and eyed her over the rim. They'd just see about that. He had a feeling that the desire they felt for each other, the need to see each other naked, was too big, too intense, for either of them to resist.

Five

Full disclosure, M, I want to sleep with you again.

Disconcerted by Mack's statement, Molly stomped through the back corridors and used the old servants' staircase to step into the sunlight through a door adjacent to the bright and lush conservatory. She knew the mansion like the back of her hand, knew where to find her favorite paintings, when the silver needing cleaning, how to access the secret passageways and the cellars, what was stored in the attic. She loved running her hands over the walls that had sheltered so many people at different times over the past century.

Right now she wasn't thinking about the history of the hotel. She was too busy trying to get some sense of her tumultuous feelings. Her dominant emotion was anger…

She was furious with Mack…

Or was she? *Really?* Maybe she was angry at herself for still wanting him so damn much, for allowing herself to feel anything other than cool disdain.

She was definitely angry with Beth. She was always mad at her family.

And she was a little upset with Jameson for being ill.

Oh, and she was also pissed that Jared, Autumn's fiancé, dumped her a couple of days before their long-planned wedding a few weekends ago. Autumn was acting like it was no big deal but Molly knew she was hurting. She had to be.

That's an awful lot of mad, Haskell.

Slumping against the back wall of the property, she pulled her phone out of the back pocket of her pants and punched in Autumn's number. She tried to check in on her best friend a couple of times a day, just to take her emotional temperature. Autumn had yet to break down, to cry, and Molly worried about her.

Autumn answered her phone and Molly asked where she was.

"Actually, I'm hiding out in the bar, trying to catch up on paperwork," Autumn told her.

Perfect. "I'll see you there soon."

The bar was a small stone building detached from the main resort, situated between the art studio and Moonlight Ridge's heated swimming pool. Modeled after an English pub, the small space was dominated by a handcrafted wooden bar, behind which sat a world-class collection of whiskeys. At ten in the morning, the place was empty of guests and staff and Molly took two bottles of water from an under-counter fridge and walked over to where her friend sat, the table in front of her piled high with paper.

Molly sat down and inspected Autumn. Her honey-colored hair was bundled up onto the top of her head and secured with a clip and her black-rimmed glasses dominated her face. She looked a little harried and a tad frustrated but nothing like an almost-jilted bride. She'd barely been able to breathe when Mack left but Autumn was acting upbeat, like her nonwedding was a brief blip on her radar.

"How are you doing, sweetie?" Molly asked her, handing her a bottle of water.

Autumn shrugged. "Fine." She gestured to the chaotic table. "I'm just trying to undo the mess not getting married created."

"Have you spoken to Jared?" Molly gently asked her.

Autumn pretended to inspect her laptop screen. "Nope. It's over. There's nothing to say."

Molly bit her lip, wondering whether to push her to open up. Autumn needed to rant and bitch, to scream and sob. Keeping all this emotion bottled up wasn't helpful or healthy. But she was also an adult and entitled to deal with her emotions any way she thought fit. "If you want to TP his house or key his car or slash his tires, I'll be there, okay?"

Autumn smiled. "Thanks, Mol. Now, what sent you running from your office? Beth or Mack?"

It was scary how well Autumn knew her. "Both," she reluctantly admitted.

Autumn rested her forearms on the table, her attention on Molly. "What happened?"

"Grant wants money to invest in some business his friend is establishing," Molly admitted. "Beth was passing along the message."

Autumn looked skeptical on hearing her brother's latest scheme. "What business?"

"Ah, that's where she got a bit vague. She knew exactly how much he needed—ten thousand—but the details around the business itself were a bit sketchy."

Autumn did a massive eye roll.

"She got a bit intense in her demands and Mack caught her looming over my desk," Molly continued. "He called her out for threatening me."

"Good for him," Autumn stated.

Molly rested her water bottle on her forehead. "My family is so messed up, Autumn, and they are damn embarrassing. Mack never liked my brothers, none of the Holloway boys did, and honestly, I can't blame them for that."

"They are toxic, Mol. They aren't good for you. And if you tell me that you are responsible for your family, then I'm going to tell you, yet again, that you're talking rubbish."

Molly looked at her friend, grateful for her fierce attitude and insane loyalty.

"They are adults, Molly. They can support themselves. It's not your job to pay their rent, or to give them money for gas or to pay off a credit

card. You've got to stop enabling them, babe."
Autumn took Molly's hands and squeezed. "Mol,
you have to cut ties with them."

Autumn would always, no matter what, be
there for her. She knew this like she knew her
own signature. Just being with Autumn helped
her remember that she would be okay, that she
had a great track record of recovering after
things went south.

"You need to get Beth out of your face and
out of this organization, Molly. She's bad news."

Molly considered her suggestion and immediately dismissed it. Beth wasn't great at her job
but Jameson's lack of systems didn't help the
situation. Beth hadn't made any huge mistakes,
and her intense dislike of the bookkeeper wasn't
enough to have her canned.

She didn't have the authority—dammit!—
to fire a senior staff member so she'd have to
take her request to Mack. It was obvious that he
didn't like Beth, but before firing her, he'd dig
deeper, scratch under the surface to understand
her motivations for wanting Beth gone, and that
would lead him to discover Molly's secret. Jameson might, one day, forgive her for stealing. But
Mack? Not a chance.

Even as a kid Mack had a code of honor, a steel rod in his backbone, lines that couldn't be crossed. Because his dad had been so unreliable and immoral, he valued truth, taking responsibility for one's choices and integrity above all else. He had incredibly high standards and, on hearing about her teenage crime, she'd fall short in his eyes.

She still couldn't bear to disappoint him, dammit.

Besides, Mack had always fought her battles as a kid, but she was an adult, and she didn't need him to do that anymore. No, Beth was her problem, her mess, and it was her job to clean it up.

"Moving on from the never delightful Beth, how is it going with Mack?" Autumn asked, curiosity on her face. "Are you still attracted to him?"

Attraction was such a tame word for her yearning and burning emotions. But basically, yes.

Hell yes.

She wanted to know what making love with him, as a grown-up, felt like. She wanted to explore that incredible body with her hands and mouth, taking time to discover all the ways he'd changed. And all the ways he'd not.

It might take some time, but Molly was very okay with that…

Lord, she was in a world of trouble.

"You are, aren't you?" Autumn crowed. Then her eyes narrowed. "Something happened," she stated.

A lot of somethings had happened… "I love you dearly, Autumn, but I don't want to discuss Mack…or not just yet," Molly said, resting her bottle of water against her forehead.

Autumn pouted, disappointment in her eyes. But because she was a lovely friend, she nodded. "Okay."

Autumn looked at her watch and sighed. "I need to head into town for a meeting with a newly engaged couple."

"Try and persuade them to have their wedding here," Molly said, standing up. Weddings brought in a lot of money and they didn't have enough booked for summer.

"I always do," Autumn said on a small shrug. "Unfortunately, the mothers of the brides love Moonlight Ridge but the brides want less country house and more cool."

It was a criticism she'd heard before and something she wanted to change. Molly walked around the table to drop a kiss on her friend's head. "Thanks for the chat."

"Anytime," Autumn replied. "Trust Mack, Mol. I really think you can."

Molly disagreed. She didn't trust anyone, except Jameson. Everyone else had, in some way or the other and to different degrees, let her down. And sometime in the future, she'd do the same to Jameson.

The thought made her want to throw up.

At around eight that night, Molly shut down her computer, finally done with the day. Not wanting to go back to an empty apartment, Molly considered visiting Jameson. But it was getting late, he would be watching TV, possibly dozing, and she didn't want to disturb him.

She stood up and walked to the window of her office, staring into the shadows down below and rested her throbbing head on the cool window. She was mentally drained and physically exhausted and the thought of dragging herself across the grounds to her apartment above the stable block was, right now, too much to contemplate.

She glanced back to look at her laptop screen

and grimaced. Having spent most of the day doing calculations and projections, she came to the unwelcome conclusion that the resort was in more trouble than even she suspected. Oh, she'd had her suspicions for a while but it was worse than she'd thought.

The reality was that they were facing the quietest summer season on record; the bookings they had wouldn't cover costs. She needed to do something to pull people in, something to bolster the cash flow. If she could get authorization to implement her ideas, she'd have a chance at saving the resort.

She couldn't let this fabulous place slide away or shut its doors. Without people, Moonlight Ridge would lose its magic.

Dammit, if only she and Jameson had discussed her plans for the resort before he got sick; that way she could instigate her strategy to revitalize Moonlight Ridge and he could concentrate on getting well.

She wanted to succeed because she loved the resort and could see its immense potential. And also because Jameson had been so good to her and she couldn't tolerate the idea of letting him down. He'd offered her a job at fourteen, paying her half her wages in cash and putting the rest into a bank account she hid from her family. In her senior year, shortly after she stole the money from him, he offered to pay for her college degree. Molly, consumed with guilt, proud and already in his debt, refused, insisting she'd apply for a dance scholarship. When she damaged her knee, she knew she'd have to find another way to fund her dream of a decent education.

The next few years had been tough but she managed, eventually returning to Asheville and sliding into a management position with Jameson.

Moonlight Ridge was still the only place she wanted to be. And if she didn't do something quickly, it would fade into obscurity. She refused to let that happen; there *had* to be something she could do.

She could ask Mack, Grey and Travis to throw some money at the problem; they were all self-made millionaires, a fact Jameson was exceptionally proud of. But even if Jameson agreed to that, and he never would, their infusion of cash would be like placing a Band-Aid on an open wound. It wasn't a long-term solution.

Molly heard the knock on her door. Sighing,

she turned and watched as Mack stepped into her office. It was brutally unfair that, at the end of a long day, he still looked as good as he did this morning. His white cotton shirt wasn't wrinkled, and his pants looked like he'd pulled them on ten minutes before. The only hint that it was the end of the day was the dark shadow of stubble on his jaw and his less-than-perfect hair.

"It's late, Molly. Time to pack it up," Mack told her, stepping into her office.

Irritation bubbled; she wasn't a child who needed to have her hours regulated. "I'm very capable of deciding when my workday should end, Holloway."

Mack sent her a sour look and dragged his hand through his thick hair. "Dammit, Mol, do you have to fight me on everything?" Mack muttered. "You have dark stripes under your eyes, you look pale and any fool can see that you are shattered. You need a good meal and a solid night's sleep. That's all I meant, for God's sake."

Molly grimaced and dropped down to sit on the edge of her two-seater couch. Resting her elbows on her knees, she sent Mack an apologetic look. "Sorry."

Mack sat down in the wingback chair opposite

her. He leaned forward and placed his big hands on her knees, and Molly felt lust and need and want flow through her body, instantly reviving her. How did he do that? And why was he the only one who could?

"Molly, look at me."

Molly lifted her eyes to connect with his, the deepest, darkest black, mysterious and rather wonderful. Mack squeezed her knees, his fingertips digging into her skin under the skirt of her figure-hugging dress. "In case nobody has said this to you lately, and I doubt they have, thank you for all your hard work and your dedication to this place. I have no doubt that Moonlight Ridge would be in a more precarious position if you weren't here, Curls."

Until Mack said the words, Molly hadn't realized how much she needed to hear them. Telling herself not to let him see how deeply his words affected her, she looked away.

There had been a lot of talk when Jameson installed her as his second in charge, Molly told him. "A lot of people thought the apple wouldn't fall far from the tree," she added.

"Jameson raised us to take responsibility for

our individual choices. Your dad's choices were his own."

As were hers.

"Besides, you're an orange, not an apple. Or, judging by your prickly attitude, a cactus," Mack commented. The flash of humor in his eyes, and the way his mouth lifted up at the corners, told her he was teasing and she remembered that, back when he was young and fun, Mack used to mess with her.

When they were much older, he took his teasing to their lovemaking, and, despite how young she'd been, it had always been a fun and loving experience.

Strange that Mack at eighteen was still the best lover she'd ever had. At thirty-three and having had some time to hone those skills, he'd be, she had no doubt, freaking amazing.

Her panties felt warm and a little damp and her nipples pushed against the lace barrier of her bra. Yep, he still could set her blood on fire.

"What were you thinking about just now?" Mack asked, lifting his hands off her knees and leaning back in his chair. He rested his hands against his flat stomach, curiosity on his face.

Molly rewound and remembered her concerns

about Moonlight Ridge. She could discuss her plans for the resort with Mack; it was a subject they had in common. And it would help her to ignore her insane sexual attraction to this infuriatingly sexy man.

"I was thinking about what we could do to improve the place."

"That's why I stopped by. I've been thinking about your top ideas and the easiest one to begin with is updating the rooms. We can get started immediately by repainting the suites and updating the linens."

Yes! She was grateful. It was a start but so much more needed to be done.

"That's a great start..." Molly's words trailed off.

"But?"

"But we still need to get to get a lot of people here, fast. Our bookings are down for the summer and we won't cover costs if we don't do something."

"Yeah, I realized that." Mack rubbed his jaw. "My brothers and I could give the resort a cash injection if it needed it."

So he'd considered that option, too. Molly was

pleased to know he was prepared to part with his cash, that he would do anything to keep Moonlight Ridge going. But as nice as that would be, it wasn't a long-term solution, as she told him. "We need guests, Mack. That's what must change. We need feet through the door."

"Let me look at the finances and see how much more money we can release to throw at a marketing campaign. Hopefully, I'll be able to make sense of the bookkeeping system. It's a goddamn mess."

Molly sympathized. "I know. Do you want some help?"

Mack nodded. "I'd like that. Do you want some help finessing your marketing ideas?"

There was so much history between them, so much pain, but she had to put that away and concentrate on what was important and that was saving Moonlight Ridge. "Yeah, we can do that."

Mack stared at her for a minute, maybe two, before standing up and placing one hand on the arm of her couch and looming over her. His penetrating eyes searched her face and, lifting his other hand, he swiped his thumb across her bottom lip. "I want my friend back, Molly. The friend I lost because I was young, dumb and an ass. And that means facing what I did and how I did it. And then I look at you and all I want is to kiss you senseless and strip you naked."

They were words she'd long thought she needed to hear; words she'd dreamed of. But they also scared her because Molly knew that it wouldn't take much for her to fall under his spell again. And she refused to do that; she didn't think she could handle Mack loving and leaving her again.

Molly resisted the urge to touch his thumb with the tip of her tongue. "Let's leave the past where it belongs, Mack."

Mack's smile was gentle and a little sad.

"Normally, I'd be the first to agree with you but with you, I can't do that."

"Mack…"

She needed to tell him, to explain that nothing was going to happen between them, that they could be colleagues who worked together and that was all. But when Mack looked at her like he was doing now, cataloging her features, soaking her in, her words stuck on her tongue.

Mack dropped a light kiss on the corner of

her mouth before pulling back to look at her. "Get some sleep, Curls. And, yes, that's a damn order."

Mack kissed her again, his mouth hard and direct, before walking away from her and out the room.

Well, okay, then.

Jameson, sitting in a comfortable chair on his expansive deck, watched Molly and Mack crossing his bright green lawn to join him, each trying so damn hard to play it cool.

Morons, he thought, chuckling. Since they first met, they'd never been able to ignore each other.

Mack was looking more relaxed, thank God. His oldest, Jameson admitted, worried him. Mack played his cards so close to his chest, and his defensive walls were sky-high. Molly had been the only person, besides him, to slip under, over or through those barriers—Travis and Grey had only gotten so far—to see that, at his heart, Mack was a man who needed to be loved, who needed love. Despite his me-against-the-world stance, more than most, Mack needed a family, a wife, a place to belong. Jameson had given him that for ten or so years but Mack had been on his own for far too long.

And Molly, God, she was the daughter of his heart. Over the years there had been so many times when he wanted to stand between her and her family, to meet with them privately and tell them to leave her the hell alone. He wasn't a fool; he knew that Molly still supplemented their income. There was no way they could enjoy the lifestyle they did without a discernible source of income. He'd hired Beth in hopes the family would leave Molly alone, but Beth was too selfish and too smart to hand over her money to her boyfriend's family. The Haskells always had money and Jameson had no doubt it was from Molly.

She was their bank manager, their personal ATM, their get-out-of-jail card.

He wouldn't have a problem with her handing over her money—it was hers after all, and she was an adult—if they treated her with an ounce of respect. But they didn't. They didn't even seem to like her much because she reminded them of what they could be, could do, if they put a little effort in, made better choices.

The tall trees, Jameson thought, always caught the wind.

Jameson felt his newspaper being plucked from his fingers and turned to see Giada standing in front of him, the now-folded paper pressed against her fantastic breasts. Jameson sighed. The last thing he should be thinking about was Giada's rack.

Then again, thinking was all he could do right now. Sex, like work, was off the table for a few more months.

Giada frowned. Her dark eyebrows pulled together and Jameson knew that she was about to deliver another lecture in her slightly accented voice, her fabulous eyes flashing with impatience. God, the woman was bossy. He rather liked it.

He'd always, terribly inconveniently, liked her. And lusted after her.

"You're reading the news," Giada complained.

Something he'd done since he was a kid. "It's called staying informed."

"It's stressful," Giada shot back. "Politics, corruption, more politics, a gruesome murder."

Jameson tipped his head back and closed his

eyes. "I do not need to be wrapped in cotton wool, woman. And give me back my cigars," he grumbled. Giada thought she was so clever in confiscating his cigars but she didn't know that he had secret stashes all over the house.

The fact that he had to resort to sneaking around to take a puff pissed him off.

Giada placed the newspaper on the side table next to him and slapped her hands on her hips. Round hips, sturdy hips…hips that could handle his broad hands on them, a body that could handle his bulk and strength, as he pushed into her.

Jameson wiped his hands over his face at the image of a naked Giada under him. There was only one thing worse than fantasizing about a woman he couldn't have and that was knowing it would be months before he could even try.

God, he was done with feeling like crap.

"What are you thinking about?" Giada demanded, her eyes drilling into him.

He'd never admit the truth so he gestured to M&M. He lowered his voice to make sure that they didn't hear him; if they did, being stubborn fools, they'd do everything in their power to prove him wrong.

"They are perfect for each other. I am so glad

he's home. She needs him and he desperately needs her."

Giada put herself between Jameson and his children. Because Molly was, in every way that counted, his. She lifted a finger and poked him in the chest, sending ribbons of electricity skating over his skin. "Do not interfere. They are adults and are perfectly capable of making their own choices and decisions."

Sure, but where was the fun in that? "I have no problem nudging them," Jameson replied.

"No nudging," Giada warned as Molly and Mack called out their greetings. As they approached, Giada sent him a victorious smile and turned to face his visitors.

Before he could greet his son and the woman he hoped would one day be his daughter-in-law, Giada spoke again. "I'm so glad you are here. I need help."

Molly bent down to kiss his cheek and when she stood up, she kept a hand on his shoulder. She looked at Giada and nodded. "What do you need? What can I do?"

Giada handed him a smile that stopped his heart. It was sexy and sneaky. And savage. "You can help me search the house for Jameson's contraband cigars."

Shee-it. Busted.

Six

Molly juggled the heavy files in her arms as they walked away from Jameson's house and back toward Moonlight Ridge, Mack carrying a heavy box of ledgers and files like it was a box of light-as-air biscuits. When Giada offered to accompany Jameson on a slow, short walk through the wild garden and back, they'd raided his study for any paperwork relating to Moonlight Ridge. There had been more than they expected.

The man, Molly decided, was strong. Like pick-me-up-and-haul-me-away strong. And yep, she was having a few fantasies of him doing exactly that. Preferably when they were both naked.

Molly dropped back a step to eye his exceedingly nice ass. Unlike so many men's butts, his wasn't flat; nor was it too round. It was just, well, *perfect*. His broad shoulders and muscular back told her that he wasn't a stranger to working out and his long, muscular thighs reminded her that he'd been, back in the day, an excellent swimmer.

Her teenage boyfriend was now a hot, sexy, powerful man. And he still managed to set her panties on fire.

Shouldn't that ship have sailed, had a mutiny, burned out and been scuttled? But no, it seemed not.

Because his butt, his entire body, just did it for her.

Mack stopped abruptly and spun around to look at her. "Are you checking out my ass?" he demanded.

Oops, busted.

Molly made a show of juggling the files in her arms. "Just trying to get a better grip on these."

Mack's eyes danced with amusement and she caught a brief flash of bright white teeth behind his blinding smile. "Liar, you were *so* checking me out."

"So checking me out..." Molly mimicked him. "You sound like a teenage girl."

"Maybe, but I'm still waiting for you to disagree."

Molly scowled at him. "Okay, princess, your ego obviously needs a bit of stroking." Her next words gushed out as she tried to imitate an over-the-top teenager. "O! M! G! You are so hot! Do you work out? Can I get your autograph? You are sooooo cute. Can I try and bounce a coin off your butt?"

Mack laughed at her, amusement making him look ten years younger. Molly stared at him, her heart thumping, as she saw, for the first time, the laughing boy she remembered. Yeah, there he was... Mack. Her friend. The boy who'd introduced her to love.

Hello...

Mack's smile faded as he tipped his head to the side. "Why are you looking at me like that?"

"Like how?"

"Like you are seeing me for the first time."

Ah, because maybe she was? Molly ignored his question and resumed walking, her arms burning. "So how do you keep that fabulous bod in great shape?" she asked, still curious. "Do you still swim?"

"No." Molly saw a flash of embarrassment hit his features and wondered what he was hiding.

"Running? Gym? Weights?"

Mack jerked his head to where a large tree stump sat in the middle of the lawn, decorated with a weathered copper birdbath. "What happened to the oak tree?"

"Big storm six months ago. The trunk cracked and it was deemed to be a safety hazard so we had to cut it down. And stop changing the subject...what do you do for exercise?"

"Yoga."

Molly wasn't sure she'd heard him right. Mack and his brothers were men's men, guys who relished close-contact sports. The nittier, grittier and dirtier, the better.

She could not imagine Mack Holloway twisting himself into a human pretzel.

"Yoga? Gentle stretching resulted in those muscles? No way!"

"I do advanced Bikram Yoga. It's intense and we practice in a hot room. It's physically demanding. Bikram Yoga is what I do religiously."

"And what do you do nonreligiously?" Molly

asked as they approached the back door to Moonlight Ridge.

Molly wasn't looking forward to trudging up all those narrow steps with her arms full of heavy ledgers.

"I also practice Krav Maga," Mack admitted.

Now that made sense. And typical Mack, he wasn't one to settle for a judo or karate class; he had to attempt to master the hardest self-defense discipline in the world.

"You're nuts."

"It's been said before," Mack said, resting his box on his knee to push open the door to let her enter the inn. "You're still in pretty good shape yourself…how do you stay so slim?" She was happy he'd noticed. But only because she wanted him to appreciate what he'd never lay hands on again.

Well, that was the plan but her body, and libido, had different ideas. It had been a long time since she'd had a man's hands on her, an awfully long time since Mack had seen her naked.

He'd been good at sex back then; she had no doubt that he'd be brilliant at it now.

Molly cursed herself as she stepped into the

inn and immediately turned right to hit the stairs. She was not going to sleep with Mack...

Absolutely, categorically, definitely...

Maybe.

Arrgh!

"You didn't answer my question, Mol," Mack said from behind her.

Ah, what had he asked? Oh, what she did to keep in shape. She looked around and shrugged. "I run up and down these steps a hundred times a day."

She resumed her climb up the familiar staircase, each crack and knot a familiar friend.

"You don't dance anymore?"

Molly immediately stiffened. She'd been waiting for him to broach the subject of her dancing, the other great passion of her teenage life.

God, everything changed after that hot, sexy summer.

"I left ballet behind a long time ago," Molly stated, her voice barely above a whisper. And God, how she missed it. She'd been, over the years, so tempted to pull on her tights and ballet pointes, wanting to do grand jetés or to pirouette across a studio.

But she'd been warned that her knee was too

weak for her to return to classical ballet so she assuaged her need for dance by joining modern dance, tap and hip-hop dance classes.

For someone who could once make her body fly, not being able to do grand jetés and grand adages was torture.

"Why?"

Molly stopped her climb and leaned her back against the cool white wall behind her. "I tore the anterior cruciate ligament in my knee. And when I say tore, I mean I ripped it to shreds."

Mack grimaced. "Nasty. What happened?"

Molly wanted to push her hair off her face but her hands were full so she resorted to trying to blow the annoying curl out of her eyes. Mack placed his box on the next stair, removed the books and files from her hands and placed them on top of his box. "Why didn't we get a porter to do the heavy lifting?" he ruefully asked.

"Because we thought Jameson would have a file, maybe two, not a truckload of paperwork."

Mack lifted his hand and with his finger, pushed her curl off her cheek and tucked it behind her ear. He looked down at her and, once again, wished she could tell what he was thinking. She didn't like being shut out, not by Mack, not by the man whom she once knew inside out. "You were telling me about your dance injury."

Molly rubbed her left wrist with the curled fingers of her right hand. When she saw Mack looking at the action, she immediately stopped. He knew it was something she did when she was feeling anxious or out of her depth.

"It was dress rehearsal and I caught my foot in my dress and I went down. I heard the pop and I knew it wasn't good. I was helped off stage and then they started phoning around for someone to pick me up and take me to the hospital."

She wouldn't tell him that, delirious with pain, she'd told them to call him, insisting that he'd come and get her. The EMS techs tried him but he hadn't answered. Then they tried her mother and her brothers, none of whom they could reach.

Eventually, it was Jameson who met her at the same hospital Travis had recently left. And he'd held her hand when they told her that dance, like Mack, would never be part of her future again.

She felt its loss like a body blow.

Molly shrugged off those bitter memories. "They did reconstructive surgery but it will never be as strong as it was so pirouettes and arabesques are solidly off-limits." She gestured to the narrow stairs above them. "So I now mostly climb stairs."

"I'm so sorry, Mol," Mack told her and her eyes burned at the emotion she heard in his voice. He'd loved to watch her practice, had encouraged her to pursue her passion when her mother and brothers dismissed her talent. He'd understood, on a fundamental level, how important it was to her…

"I do still dance, modern and hip-hop mostly, but it's not the same. I loved ballet."

"I know," Mack said, looking and sounding serious.

"Yeah, well, hell happens," Molly said, ducking behind flippancy.

"Yeah, it really does," Mack said, his hand cupping her cheek, his thumb sliding over her cheekbone. His eyes drifted over her face, his stern mouth relaxed. "At seventeen I thought you the most beautiful creature I'd ever set eyes on. But you are lovelier today than you were back then. It's blowing my mind."

Molly rested her palms flat against the wall behind her, watching as his mouth descended toward hers. He smelled different, Molly thought, his scent more subtle but powerful, a dizzying combination of citrus and spice. His beard was stronger, his cheekbones more defined, those eyes shuttered, but God, his lips, when they touched hers, were still the same. A little sweet, a little soft, devastating and demanding at the same time. Mack placed his thumb on her chin, an unmistakable command for her to open up so she did, letting him slide inside.

Unable to stop herself, Molly placed her hands on the balls of his shoulders, feeling his heat beneath the material of his casual, expensive shirt. As he took a long, languid discovery of her mouth, she ran her hands down his arms, feeling the bumps of those impressive muscles, the raised veins in his forearms. Needing to explore herself, she slid her hands across his wide, hard chest and danced her fingers over his ladderlike stomach, until she hit the button of his jeans. Later, she wouldn't be able to decide whether she touched accidentally or on purpose, but when the side of her hand brushed his erection, she heard his swift intake of breath.

Mack whipped his head up, stared at her, his eyes wild and wicked and then his mouth, hot, sensual and rather wonderful, covered hers again. This time he used his big body to gently press her against the wall, and while his tongue was dancing with hers, she released a breathy moan. His scent rolled over her, earthy and primal and hot as fire. Molly gripped his shirt, twisting the material as he dragged his stubble across her jawline, stopping to pull her earlobe into his mouth. A little tease and a little taste and he was off exploring again, his mouth trailing down her neck, nudging aside the material of her loose silk T-shirt to expose the skin of her shoulder.

They shouldn't be doing this; it was a lethal game. They were tempting a tornado, flirting with a firestorm. Too much had happened between them—hurt, anger and disappointment—but Molly couldn't force herself to verbalize the words that would make her drop out of the game.

Desire shimmered between them, hot and feral and uncontrollable. If she made the slightest move, if she gave in to temptation and allowed her hands to roam, her mouth to feast, she'd tumble into a situation that would spin, rapidly she was sure, out of her control.

It took everything she had to stand still, to harness herself...

"Come on, Curls, give me something. Anything," Mack muttered against her lips, his teeth gently nipping her bottom lip.

It was that small bite, that sexy nip, that shattered her control. Swamped and slapped by passion, she gripped his shirt, twisted it and pulled her to him, feeling his hard body pushing her to the wall again. Her tongue slipped into his mouth, and he moaned when she feasted on him, needing more, needing everything.

She'd missed this; she'd missed him. He knew how to touch her—his hand on her breast, capturing her nipple between his thumb and finger proved that—knew when to advance, how to retreat. Molly sighed when his hard shaft pressed against the juncture of her thighs and, oblivious to where they were, she opened her legs to give him better access. Frustrated, she lifted her knee to curl her leg behind his thigh, thanking God she was still ballet flexible. Mack's hand ran up and down the back of her thigh, his fingers curling inward, coming dangerously close to her happy spot. Mack bent and held the backs of her thighs, easily lifting her, and it was the most natural thing in the world to wind her legs around his trim waist, to hook her ankles in the small of his back.

They were groping on the back stairway of Moonlight Ridge and she didn't care. At all.

They shared another hot, hard and wild kiss and Molly lifted her hips to scrape her core against his erection. Man, he felt so good. Nothing made sense but for them to get naked, immediately.

The slam of a door below them made them flinch, and the sound of heavy footsteps on the stairs below them, a floor down, had Molly dropping her legs and Mack bending to pick up the heavy box to hide his erection.

As the footsteps reached them, they continued their slow walk up the stairs, standing to the side to allow the fit, and young, porter to pass them.

Neither of them looked at each other; they didn't speak.

And when they hit their floor, Mack pealed left to go to his office and she went right to hers.

But really, the only place she wanted to be was in his bed.

Molly left her apartment around nine and walked through the soft, fragrant night, navigating her way to the guesthouse by the light of the moon. Since their hot kiss on the stairs,

Molly felt hot and horny, and she was sick of waiting for him to come to her so she'd decided to take the initiative.

But what if he'd changed his mind? Molly winced. She was ninety percent sure he wouldn't; his kiss had been demanding and ferocious.

You're overthinking this, Haskell. Just tell him you want a one-night stand and see what he says.

Molly looked over her shoulder and considered retracing her steps back to her place. Good girls didn't ask for sex; men should make the first move...

Molly released a silent curse, annoyed that she was listening to the old-fashioned voice in her head. She was a woman in her early thirties. She was allowed to want sex. It was a natural, biological urge and she was single. Mack wasn't married, engaged or in, as far as she knew, a relationship. If they ended up in bed, and there were no guarantees that would happen, she wouldn't be doing anything wrong.

They were both adults...

She could have sex with him without needing a commitment, without expectations. That was what modern, emancipated women did these days and, as far as she knew, she was one of the tribe.

So then why did she feel nervous, like her heart was about to bounce out of her chest and roll around on the floor?

Molly halted at the bottom of the short steps that led up to the porch on the guesthouse of what used to be her old home.

Would this be a one-night stand? Or would they keep sleeping together until he left? What if he didn't want her…?

For God's sake, Haskell, stop! She'd seen the attraction and desire in Mack's eyes; there was no doubt that he'd be fully on board with her idea. They'd sleep together, have a fun time and they either would, or wouldn't, have sex again. Either way, she'd be fine.

She could do this.

She *would* do this. *So move your feet, Molly.*

"What are you doing, Curls?"

Mack's voice, drifting over in the darkness, wrapped around her like a warm, sensual piece of silk. Molly squinted through the darkness. His vague outline told her that he was sitting in one of the big, comfy chairs in the corner of the veranda.

"I'm not actually sure," Molly said, annoyed to hear the tremble in her voice.

"Then why don't you come up here and we can figure it out together?" Mack suggested in that low, sexy voice.

Molly walked up the steps and crossed the veranda to where he was sitting. When she reached him, his hand wrapped around her wrist and he tugged her to stand between his thighs.

Molly looked down at his masculine face, wreathed in shadows, and shuddered when his hands moved to her hips and he rested his forehead on her stomach. "I want to take you to bed, Molly."

So direct, so...adult. But could she do this... could she sleep with him and keep it simple? She was desperate to believe that she could keep all the messy emotions out of it. But this wasn't any man; this was Mack and he was, always had been, hard to resist. As kids, they'd shared a powerful connection, and she'd loved him with an intensity that still, even in hindsight, scared her. When he moved on, her heart died.

Her body was demanding sex but her mind kept insisting that getting naked with him was dangerous. He called to her; he always had. And not only because he had the face and body that could stop traffic at a hundred yards. No, she liked his scalpel-sharp mind, the way his feelings ran deep, his loyalty to Jameson. She liked the way his focus sharpened when something caught his interest, his offbeat and dry sense of humor and his calm confidence.

Mack tugged her down so that she sat astride his thighs. His mouth touched hers and something fierce, primal and deeper than attraction flared between them as Molly fell into his kiss. One arm tightened around her waist and his hand held the back of her head as if she might—crazy thought—consider removing herself from his embrace.

Mack's hand drifted over her hips, down her thighs, slid under the soft cotton of her dress and curled around the back of her knee. "What do you say, sweetheart?"

She made herself say the words, to remind herself that this could never be more than some bed-based fun. "A few hours, no expectations and no drama?"

"Works for me," Mack said, his skilled hands running up the backs of her bare thighs and flirting with the curve of her butt cheek. Mack's fingers slid under the band of her bikini panties, a small promise of what was to come.

Molly expected him to stand up, to lead her through the house to the main bedroom, to the room her parents used—thankfully redecorated—but Mack surprised her by keeping her on his lap, her knees on either side of his strong thighs. He reached up to hold her nape, gently pulling her down so that their lips could meet, and his kiss was tender, sweeter than she expected.

She expected…she didn't know what she expected, Molly thought as his skilled tongue played with hers. She'd expected assertive and confident, a little crazy, but his kiss was an exploration, a rediscovery. Sexy, hot, a little sweet.

Molly needed to touch him so she placed her hands on his chest, feeling hard muscle under her hands and she sighed, her lips opening to allow that puff of air to escape. Mack used the opportunity to slide his tongue between her lips. A flame immediately rushed along the detonator cord and ignited a fireball of crazy want and need. Molly slid down his thighs, pressed her breasts into his chest and her hips met his, her core coming to rest against his steel-hard erection.

Perfect.

As their kiss deepened, became wilder and wetter, their hands skated from body part to body part, searching for skin. Mack shifted forward in the chair, perched on the end and dragged her dress up her butt, and Molly felt the warm night air on her lower back. His hand slid down the back of her panties to cup her bare ass. Needing to touch him, she pulled Mack's shirt out of his pants to run her hands up the dip of his spine, over his muscled back, slowly making her away around to his ladderlike stomach. She could feel her heart thumping erratically, or was that Mack's?

She didn't know and it didn't matter; all that was of importance was that he was as out of control as she was. Molly ground herself against his shaft, desperate to be rid of the barriers between him.

Mack's hand covered her breast and soon his mouth was there, too, sucking her through her dress and bra. Frustrated, he pulled her dress down and then the bra cup, and dragged his hot tongue across her nipple.

Moisture flooded her panties and Molly knew

that, just by riding his shaft and having him tongue her breasts, she could come.

"You are so damn sexy, Curls," Mack muttered against her skin.

And in his arms she felt sexy, a little wild, a pagan goddess intent on pleasure. Molly whimpered when Mack's hand dived between her thighs to pull the seam of her panties to one side so that he could stroke her bare, throbbing flesh. He rubbed his thumb across her bundle of nerves and she tipped her head back. The world narrowed to his touch and he slid one finger inside her, then another.

Molly, insensible to the fact that she was half-dressed, that her breasts were bare to the night air, closed her eyes, swept away on a rising tide of passion. Mack knew exactly how to touch her; she was so close to gushing all over his fingers, to spinning away on a whirlwind of sensation.

And he was still fully dressed...

She needed more so she forced herself to slide back, her hands going to the button on his shorts, flipping it open. With hands that were very out of practice, she slid down his zipper, needing to feel his silky shaft in her hands. For him to be inside her...

Molly freed him from his underwear and shifted so that her core was riding his shaft. She groaned, tilted her hips and released a small scream when pleasure ricocheted through her.

"Want you, want you, want you," Molly chanted, feeling fireworks building behind her eyes as she rubbed his shaft. "Mack, I'm so damn close."

"I know, Mol. Use me, any way you want to." She wanted him inside her but she didn't want to stop doing this, either. She was one move, maybe two, from the most delicious orgasm and, because it had been so long, she couldn't stop. Didn't want to…

"Use me, sweetheart."

She'd be happy to. Molly ground down on him, pushing herself down, wishing she could fall into him. Working her hand between them, she palmed him, amazed at the warmth they generated. Another slide, another kick of pleasure, and Molly groaned when Mack lifted his hips to increase the pressure. She looked down into his eyes, saw the pain and pleasure on his face, and dipped her head so that her mouth could meet his. Mack stabbed her mouth with his tongue, echoing the rhythm down below, and Molly knew that she was nanoseconds from coming.

"Harder, baby, yeah, that's it."

Molly rocked herself against his shaft and everything coalesced into a thin, pulsing band of pleasure. She felt her womb contract, the gush of heat and she spun away, lying as pleasure overtook her. She felt Mack surge against her, felt his body tense and his masculine and hot release.

Molly slumped against him, his arms tightened around her, and she buried her face in his neck as her nerve endings buzzed. As the roaring in her ears subsided, she heard Mack's erratic breathing and his superfast heartbeat.

Feeling like she was losing the feeling in her trapped hand, she pulled it out from between them and scooted off his lap, turning away to rearrange her clothing and underwear.

When she turned back, Mack was dressed and his expression had returned to impassivity.

He probably had encounters like this all the time. Unlike her, he wasn't an inexperienced, churning, electrified mess of need and want and hormones.

Molly shoved her hands into her hair, wishing she knew what to say, how to act. They hadn't made love, in the traditional sense, but she did feel like Mack had taken her apart and slapped her back together again. She wasn't who she was before. She was a little off balance, felt different.

If she felt like this now, how would she feel after they made love?

Mack stood up, held out his hand to her and sent her a smile. "Come to bed with me, Mol. Since we've both taken the edge off, I want to take my time rediscovering every inch of you."

Saying no wasn't an option; she needed to be with him, in every way, so Molly put her hand in his and followed him inside the house.

Seven

Mack heard the beat-up truck long before it arrived. Standing on the driveway at the bottom of the steps leading up to the portico, he—and two guests who'd just arrived in the latest Mercedes AMG—turned to watch the truck emerge from the tree-lined driveway.

Mack stiffened as he recognized Grant and Vincent Haskell, Molly's brothers, and his least favorite people. Jerking the truck to a stop a few inches behind the Mercedes, giving the couple near heart failure, the two brothers looked at Mack through the cracked windscreen, sizing him up.

Oh, crap. Trouble had arrived.

Mack turned to look at the couple who was eyeing Molly's brothers with obvious distaste. He gestured for the porter to lead them inside. Despite not having had any contact with Molly's siblings for fifteen years, he knew, thanks to their belligerent expressions and annoyed eyes, they were happy to cause a scene.

Mack knew, via Jameson, since Molly refused to discuss her family, that they'd been banned from the property years ago and had been told if they returned, they'd be charged with trespassing. Something must've happened for them to take that risk...

Mack hoped Molly's mom was okay. Vivi wasn't a great mom but she was the only one Molly had.

Mack spread his feet apart, kept his arms loose and ready—the Haskell brothers were volatile, threw punches without thinking and the blood between them had always been bad—and watched as the two men left their vehicle.

"Holloway," Vince said, folding beefy arms over his chest. "I'm looking for my sister."

Mack kept his expression bland. "You're trespassing," he stated. "Leave now and I won't press charges."

Grant's chin jutted out, his blue eyes cold as ice. Mack could cope with Vinny, he had an impetuous temper, but Grant worried him. Even as a kid, he showed no remorse and worse, no empathy. Grant's favorite hobby was tormenting Molly. He loved, and lived for, seeing her cry.

Mack was quite sure nothing had changed.

"Molly isn't taking our calls and we need to talk to her." Grant looked at him, smiled and shrugged. "Our mom's sick and Molly needs to know."

Bullshit. In triplicate. He wasn't buying that, not for a minute, but before he could give them another chance to leave, he heard the front door open behind him. Turning, he watched Molly fly down the steps, her eyes full of fear.

Still.

The Haskell boys had gone back to hassling Molly after he'd left town; that much was obvious. In his quest to put distance between him and the accident, he'd left her to fend for herself. Mack tasted remorse at the back of his throat and glared at the two men. Brothers were supposed to protect their sisters, not tease or torment them. A part of Mack wanted to taunt them, to force them into throwing a punch, purely so that he could beat the snot out of them. With his Krav Maga training, he no longer needed his brothers for backup and could take them with one hand tied behind his back.

For every insult they tossed at her face, every demand they made on Molly, he'd make them pay.

Molly skidded to a stop beside him and slapped her hands on her hips, undiluted fury replacing fear. "Why are you here and why did you park here? We have guests arriving, you idiots!"

Grant shrugged. "Saw Holloway, wanted to say hello."

Mack called BS. Again.

"You are not allowed here, you know that! You've been banned from the property!" Molly reminded them. "Get in your truck and go before someone calls the cops."

"I'd be happy to do that," Mack growled.

"Not helping, Holloway," Molly snapped. She pointed to the truck. "Go! Now!"

"Need to talk to you," Grant said, hooking his thumbs into the pockets of his grimy jeans. "You're not answering our calls so we came out here."

"I'm busy, dammit!" Molly snapped.

"Still need to talk," Grant stated, his eyes growing colder. Mack felt the hair on the back of his neck rising and searched for some sort of emotion in his eyes and found nothing. He knew that Grant wouldn't move until he was damn well ready to.

Molly, obvioulsy coming to the same conclusion, hauled in a deep breath. "Okay, I'll hear what you have to say but not here." She gnawed at her bottom lip. "I'll meet you at the old barn near the entrance in ten minutes and we can talk."

Grant stared at her before nodding. A smile, if one could call it that, lifted the edges of his lips up. "Fine. But if you don't arrive, you know what's going to happen, right?"

Mack didn't need to see the color draining from her face to know Grant had just threatened her. He stepped forward, his hands bunched. Before he could speak, Molly lifted her arm to slap her hand against his chest, halting his progress. "I've got this, Mack. Please don't make it worse." Molly looked at her brother. "Ten minutes. I'll see you there."

Grant sneered. "Make it five. And you know

what we need so bring that, too," Grant said before catching Vinny's eye. "Let's go, dude."

Mack watched them until the rust bucket disappeared from view. When he thought his temper was vaguely under control, he turned to talk to Molly, wanting to know why she was still interacting with her waste-of-oxygen brothers.

But Molly was gone.

Damn, the girl could move fast.

Molly, standing next to Vincent's truck, darted a look toward Mack, who watched from his seat on a dirt bike he'd commandeered from Moonlight Ridge.

He'd pulled up behind her golf cart a few minutes after she approached her brothers, who were still sitting in their vehicle, and she was glad that she had some sort of backup. Her brothers had never physically hurt her, but from a young age, she knew that Grant wanted to. He'd bullied her mercilessly as a kid, but he'd never quite crossed the line into violence.

But the urge was there.

"This is all the money I have," Molly warned them, nodding at the envelope of cash. "And you should know that the next time you put a foot on this property, I will have you arrested."

Grant laughed at her. "You can do that but if you do, we won't have any reason to keep your secret, will we?"

This. Always this. She was the girl who'd called wolf once, or a few times, too often. They didn't believe that she'd cut ties with them because she hadn't followed through. And that was on her...

God, she couldn't keep living this way, feeling like the sky was about to fall on her head. She needed to confess, but Jameson couldn't take any stress so she couldn't, not yet. Not until he was a lot better.

Not only would her news upset him but she'd probably lose her job. And that would mean he'd stress about having a new manager running his beloved resort when he should be relaxing.

No, there were reasons to keep the truth from him for a little longer...

Molly scowled. "And, God, stop talking about me to your girlfriend, Grant! What the hell were you thinking, telling Beth about what happened back then? Life is tough enough without you making it a lot more difficult!"

Grant rested his arm along the back of the

bench seat. "But I like making your life miserable, Molly. You should know that by now. Thanks for the cash but we need more. We'll see you soon."

Molly watched their truck roll away and resisted the urge to rub her eye sockets with the balls of her hands. She wanted to cry, to howl, to stamp her feet and beat her fists on the ground, but Mack was watching so she couldn't indulge in an old-fashioned hissy fit.

Damn him. What did he think he was doing following her down here? She was an adult and fully able to deal with her brothers on her own.

Molly stomped over to him, feeling her temper bubble. Before she could speak, Mack did. "Please tell me that there wasn't money in that envelope, Mol."

He was really going to lecture her on what she did with her money, how she dealt with her brothers? The sheer nerve of the man. "Why are you here, Mack? This was my private business."

Mack didn't look remotely embarrassed about sticking his nose in where it didn't belong. "If you think I was going to let you confront those two on your own, then you are nuts."

Really? Now he was getting protective? "I've

been dealing with them on my own for a long time, Holloway."

She'd been spoiled in those years before Mack left. She'd not only had Mack as a backup, but Travis and Grey, too. They'd been her own little protection crew and her brothers, mostly, left her alone. They'd hassled her for a year and a bit, until she left for college. On returning to Asheville, she'd thought it was all behind her, that she and her family could find a better way forward, that they had to change the dynamic between them. She'd invited them out for a meal and told them, as kindly as she could, that she was done supporting them and they had to do without her financial contribution.

Her mom's response was to tell her, blatantly and without remorse, that she had a choice: she could either keep feeding them money or she'd go to Jameson and tell him about the money Molly stole from him. Vivi insisted Jameson wouldn't care that she had a valid reason for doing what she did. And, because her father stole from Jameson, he'd never trust her again. He might even press charges against her...

That day Molly learned from whom Grant inherited his ruthlessness. And her last ounce of respect for her mother evaporated. But a small part of her, tiny but loud, still wanted to be part of a family, to not be on the outside looking in.

Molly drilled her finger into Mack's big biceps. "Stay out of my personal business, Holloway."

Mack's eyes flashed with anger. "They were on my property, Molly."

"Your property?" Molly released a high laugh. "Your property? Are you kidding me? You haven't spent more than a night here for years, Mack!"

Mack ran a hand through his hair. "Okay, if you want to be pedantic, then it's my father's property. My dad's land, his business, his hotel. I'm just here to look after it while he's sick."

Molly watched as Mack climbed off the dirt bike. God, she was so tired. She was done with fighting, with the stress, with waiting for the shoe to drop, the sky to fall in. She was done. She just wanted it over.

Mack's hands settled on her arms and Molly forced herself to look up into his face, trying to work out what he was thinking. She hated that he managed to keep his thoughts from her, and that she'd lost the ability to read him.

But his touch was gentle, his anger gone. Mack

rubbed his hands up and down her arms to comfort her, before pulling her close and embracing her, holding her tight. She tried to pull away but Mack held her tighter, dropping his head to place his mouth by her ear. "Let me hold you, Mol, because, God, you need someone to."

Molly stopped resisting, his words touching her deep in her soul. Needing to lean on him, just for a minute, she rested her cheek against his chest and hung on, desperately trying to suck in his strength.

She was so tired of being alone.

Molly felt the burn of tears in her eyes, the tightness in her throat. She couldn't cry now; if she started she doubted she'd stop. But despite her best efforts, her tears started to fall...

And then she started to sob...

Mack came from a family of men who seldom cried. Emotions were expressed by yelling, by slamming doors and, with his brothers, an occasional clout around the head or a fight outside. Sarcasm and shouting, punches and pranks, yes...tears?

Hell, no!

He didn't know how to deal with this outpouring of…whatever was causing Molly to fall apart in his arms. Oh, her brothers were pricks, but Molly had never reacted like this, not even when her brothers decapitated her Barbie dolls or tore pages out of her beloved books. Molly was a fighter, strong as hell, and to hear her sobs coming from a place deeper than pain, scared the crap out of him.

What was going on with her?

Oh, he knew she was a workaholic and a perfectionist and that she had an overdeveloped sense of responsibility. Had her long work hours caught up with her? Were her brothers the final straw of what had been a long few weeks and months? Was she worried about Jameson? Had his return stressed her out?

What was going on behind her pretty eyes and underneath her gorgeous hair? He needed to know. Because, God, he needed to fix this. As quick as he could. Because he'd still do pretty much anything for Molly.

She was still, despite years and time and distance, his best friend.

And the woman he very badly wanted to see naked again. And as soon as possible.

However, this wasn't the time to think about

the way she smelled—delicious—the way she tasted—fantastic—and the low, breathy, soft moans she made when she came.

Wrong time, wrong place, Holloway. Get your act together.

They weren't far from the steel bridge and if they crossed it, it was a short walk to the pond. The pond was their special place, where Mack taught her how to skip stones and to swim. On the banks of that pretty pond, sitting on the branches of the cypress tree hanging over the edge of the pond and later in the treehouse he'd built with his brothers, they'd shared their fears, their deepest desires, their dreams and their hopes.

It was where they'd lost their virginity that summer night… He'd been so damn nervous, in awe of her and the passion between them.

If there was one place on the property he could get Molly to talk, the pond was it.

Ten long minutes later Mack sat on a cushion on the smooth deck of the fantastic treehouse that had replaced the one he and his brothers built as teenagers. Following Molly up the spiral staircase, he took in the cheerful interior complete with a comfortable couch, easy chairs and a galley kitchen. Beyond the lounge was a bed-room and a bathroom, and a wraparound deck gave them three-sixty views of the pond and the mountains. Where they sat was directly over the pond, and a misstep could result in a dip right into it.

It was fabulous.

Mack looked at Molly, who'd stopped crying but her face was still pale, her eyes fixed on the clear water of the pond below. "When was this built?"

"Five years ago. We thought it would be a fun place for teenagers to camp out on summer nights," she said with a shrug.

Mack nodded to the open deck and the lack of a safety railing. "Isn't that a safety violation?"

"The contractor fell ill before he could fin-ish the job and since there has not been a single booking for the treehouse in all that time, we haven't bothered to get it fixed. I think I'm the only one who ever spends any time here."

"I should get back to work," she added, a few minutes later.

She'd said variations of the same sentence five times since she stopped crying and, just like before, Mack ignored this version, too. She'd bitched about taking the time, about coming to the pond, but Mack ignored all her protestations. He was going to discover what was going on with Molly Haskell and if that meant keeping her in this treehouse for the foreseeable future, that was what he'd do.

Mack stared at her lovely profile, her skin still a little blotchy from her earlier bout of tears.

"Spill, Haskell," he told her.

Molly turned her face to him and lifted her eyebrows, trying to hit arrogance and missing by a country mile. "Excuse me?"

Mack ignored her frigid voice. "What's going on with you?" Her mouth opened and he carried on speaking before she could. "And don't you dare tell me *nothing*!"

"I'm not sure what you are talking about, Mack. I apologize for crying earlier."

Okay, they'd start there. "So why were you crying?"

Molly turned her attention back to the water. "I'm a little tense."

Pfft. "Nice try, Curls. You're not a little tense. You are massively *stressed*. You work insane hours. You don't stop. You have no social life and rarely leave the premises. I thought I was committed to my job but you're twice the work-aholic I am."

"Jameson is sick. I've been trying to do his work as well as mine," Molly said, defensively.

"But I'm here now and one of the reasons for me being here is to take the pressure off you. That hasn't happened and I'm wondering why not. Have you always been like this?"

"I work hard. It's what I do."

Mack recalled the occasional comment Jameson had made about Molly over the years; how he worried about her, that she pushed herself too hard, that she thought she owed him the world. She was overqualified and could be climbing the corporate ladder at another company. Jameson was convinced the resort was too laid-back for her.

Jameson, he suddenly realized, had been worried about Molly for a long, long time.

Seeing the stubborn look on Molly's face, he knew that he was venturing down a closed-off path. Hoping to catch her off guard, Mack changed tack.

"Why the hell are you still giving your brothers money, Mol?"

Molly's head snapped up, her delicious curls

bouncing with the sharp movement. Molly sent him a cold look. "Mind your own business, Holloway."

Not a chance. Because her business was starting to become his. Whatever made Molly sad, mad or crazy was his problem to solve. Not because she couldn't—Molly was one of the most capable, independent people he knew—but because he cared for her. She'd been a part of his childhood, had been and was still, his best friend, the person who knew him best. He was also her lover and was, and always would be, protective of her.

Nobody messed with Molly.

"They are adults, Mol, and shouldn't be asking their baby sister to bail them out."

Mack, watching her body language, saw the tension seep back into her body. It was in the way her hands tightened, in her suddenly clenched toes, the way her back hunched over.

Oh, yeah, her family was a major cause of stress. They always had been but this was harder and deeper than before.

"God, Molly, talk to me. You know you can!"

"I don't know that, Mack!" Molly responded, her tone sharp. "How can I trust anything you say? You said you'd love me forever but you left me, without a word. Without a goodbye or an explanation. *You. Left. Me.*"

Mack sighed. He'd been thinking about this lately; being back in Asheville had forced him to dig a little deeper into the past and his actions. He was big on control; there was no getting around that, but his need to protect was almost as strong.

And Molly had always been under his protection.

Mack leaned forward, captured her chin in his hand and gently pulled her on it, forcing her to meet his eyes. "I left you without a word because I knew that if you asked me to stay, if you asked if you could come with me, I would've said yes, either way. And neither of those options was best for you, Molly. You needed to stay. You needed to be in school. You needed to dance, if you'd left with me you would've given up all of that!"

"I—"

"I couldn't stay. I was, in a clumsy, crazy way, trying to protect you because I could never say no to you, Mol."

And he probably still couldn't. Mack knew that no matter what Molly asked him now, there was a good chance he'd move heaven and earth to give it to her.

She was that important to him.

Mack allowed his thumb the pleasure of drifting over her full bottom lip. "I would've given you anything you wanted, Mol. But right now I want something from you."

Molly's green eyes turned wary. "What?"

Mack kept his fingers on her face so that she kept looking at him. "I want you to trust me, Molly. I want to know what's driving you, what's hurting you, what's making you crazy. And, God, if you tell me *nothing*, I swear I'll boot you off this deck."

It was an idle threat but Molly seemed to take it seriously, possibly because he'd tossed her into this pond a hundred times when they were kids. Molly brushed an irritating curl out of her eyes before scowling at him. "You play dirty, Holloway."

Ah, but he wasn't playing at all. Not this time.

Could she trust him? Could she share her deepest secret with him? She was so damn tired, a battery whose energy was slowly being drained, with no hope of been recharged. She felt lonely and sad, and hostile, angry and guilty.

Yet, a part of her, *most* of her, would prefer to live like that to avoid seeing the same expression she remembered seeing on Jameson's face when she was six and dealing with her dad's betrayal: confusion, pain, disappointment and anguish jumping in and out of his eyes.

She'd been so young yet she understood, at a fundamental level, that her father's actions had eviscerated Jameson.

And when he'd hear about her theft, she'd be reopening, deepening and expanding that wound.

If she didn't tell him, she'd slowly fade away. If she did, she'd lose everything she loved. It was a hell of a choice…

Molly tipped her head to the side, considering the idea of telling Mack, thinking he could be her trial run for telling Jameson. Mack would be horrified and wouldn't want anything to do with her; he'd immediately hit the brakes on their relationship—if that was what it was—and start backing away. And yeah, that would suit her because a) she didn't have the strength to walk away from Mack on her own and b) at least she'd see this split coming and could be, somewhat, prepared for it.

After calling her a thief and a dozen other names—all of which she'd called herself over the years—Mack would reject her and walk out of her life. His dislike and disgust would prepare her for losing Jameson's love and support.

She hoped.

Should she do it? Could she do it? Molly didn't know.

After a few minutes more of silence, she looked at Mack, knowing her expression was granite-hard. "If I tell you something, do you promise not to tell Jameson?"

Mack's eyes darted across her face as if he was trying to judge how serious she was being. "What could be so bad that you can't tell my dad? He adores you."

Right now he did. When her secret came out, Jameson would look at her the same way he looked at her father, with confused disgust.

"Jameson can't handle stress right now so I need you to promise not to tell him." Once Mack gave his word, he never reneged on it.

"Are you, or is he, in danger or in legal jeopardy?" Mack demanded.

"No."

Mack nodded. "Then I promise."

She couldn't believe that she was finally going to allow her secret to see the light of day. Molly sucked in a deep breath, knowing that her life, from this point on, would change again, that she was all but pushing Mack through the door, ending whatever it was they'd managed to find again.

And that was okay; it was going to happen at some point so it might as well be now, when the pain was anticipated and manageable.

"A few weeks after you left, my mother was out of money and we were about to be evicted. She kept asking me to get the money from Jameson. I was desperate. They were pressurizing me and I didn't want to have to move again so I stole two thousand dollars from Jameson. It was the end of my shift, he'd gone to visit Travis and I went into his office and took it from the Chinese tea caddy on the windowsill behind his desk."

Mack's expression didn't change. He just looked at her, his face inscrutable. In searching his eyes, she didn't see disgust or anger, just curiosity.

"That's my big secret." Molly shrugged. "My

family knows I took the money and whenever I don't do what they want, that is, when I balk at giving them money, they threaten to tell Jameson."

"Nice," was Mack's only response.

Molly frowned, confused. "Okay, you can start yelling now."

"Why would I yell at you, Molly?"

Was he messing with her? "I *stole* money from *your* dad, just like my dad stole money from him. I've never come clean, never told him, never confessed."

Mack nodded, obviously agreeing with her. "No, you didn't do any of those things. But from what Jameson told me, you did refuse to let him pay for college for you, choosing instead to work your butt off to get a scholarship and working as a bartender to put yourself through school. And then, instead of joining a corporate company, you came back to Moonlight Ridge to work for Jameson, to work your *ass* off for Jameson."

His next words nearly knocked her off the deck. "Your actions speak far louder than words, Mol, and they reflect your remorse."

Molly just stared at him, still waiting for him to castigate her, to yell and scream at her.

"Why didn't you hunt Jameson down and ask him for the cash? He would've given it to you, no questions asked." Mack bent his knee, placing his forearm on it.

Good question. "He was so stressed, Mack. You'd left and he was so worried about you. Grey was spending more and more time with friends, and Travis was angry and dispirited. And still in the hospital." She bit her lip. "He looked gray and tired, as if another crisis would drop him to his knees. I tried, for a couple of days, to ask him but he was snappy and brusque and then we were told we were getting kicked out…"

"So you just took it."

She didn't want to put lipstick on a pig. "I didn't take it, Mack, I *stole* it."

Mack acknowledged her words with a slight dip to his head. "Why didn't you tell Jameson at some point? I mean, with a decent conversation, you could've averted a lot of stress and anxiety. And told your brothers to go to hell, which had to be a great incentive."

Ah, another great question. And one that would be so much more difficult to answer. Molly rested her chin on her bent knee. "I came back to the resort as a penance, I suppose. I wanted Jameson to see how hard I worked, that I could do a good job so that when I told him, because I've always planned to, he'd take that into consideration when he was debating whether to fire me or not. But I love it here, Mack. I love working here."

She really did. Moonlight Ridge was her place, where she belonged.

"I don't think he would've fired you, Mol."

"I'm my father's daughter, Mack. He was a thief and now I am one, too. My mother is a perpetual victim and I've just given my brothers money, not knowing what they are going to do with it. Buy drugs or guns, play blackjack, who the hell knows? I don't ask and they don't tell me. That's the family I come from."

"But it's not who *you* are."

"It's not who you want me to be but yes, it is who I am," Molly stated.

"I was supposed to have a meeting with Jameson, the day he had his brain episode," Molly continued her explanation. "We were going to discuss the resort and I was going to tell him everything, come clean. I knew he would fire me. Stealing is the line you can't cross with Jameson.

I'd saved enough to rent an apartment, to pay for movers, to reestablish myself. I was going to break ties with my family, to start again…"

"But then he ended up in the hospital."

"Yeah, and I'm back to where I was. I can't tell him. I can't afford to stress him out. But I will tell Jameson at some point, I have to." Molly looked him in the eye, straightened her shoulders and lifted her chin. "You have Jameson's full authority to act on his behalf, so what are you going to do?"

Mack lifted his hands, looking confused. "About what?"

"About me, you idiot! Are you going to fire me?"

"I am not firing you because you did something stupid when you were under pressure and were a kid! That's between Jameson and you, Molly."

Molly's shoulders dropped and a little tension slid away. "Will you tell Grey and Travis?" she asked in a small voice.

Mack shook his head. "What part of *that's between you and Jameson* did you not understand, Mol?"

A curious combination of hope, relief and astonishment flowed through her. "I didn't expect you to react like this, Mack. I expected—"

Mack waited for her to finish her sentence but when she just shook her head, he filled the silence. "You forget that I know you, Mol. I know who you are beneath your spreadsheets and your lists, your constant push for perfection—"

"The accounting system is far from perfect."

"The accounting system is a freakin' mess but that's not on you. That was Jameson's responsibility and Beth's." Mack stared at her before shaking his head. "She's not only shitty at her job but she has questionable taste in men, too, if she's dating your brother."

Molly handed him a small smile. "You're not wrong."

Mack stood up and offered Molly a hand to pull her up. "I seldom am."

Mack turned to walk off the deck but Molly's hand on his elbow stopped his progress. He looked over his shoulder at her and raised his eyebrows.

She swallowed and rapidly blinked, trying to disperse the sheen of tears in her eyes. "Thank you. For believing in me."

Mack touched her cheek with gentle fingers. "Oh, Mol. You are so damn tough on yourself."

Molly's eyes connected with his. "And you aren't?"

"Touché. We are, in so many ways, our own worst enemies." Mack held out his hand and Molly slid her fingers between his, feeling for the first time in forever, a little hopeful, optimistic.

Maybe, just maybe, there was a tiny chance the sky wouldn't fall on her head.

Because Jameson's office was next to hers and only thin drywall separated the two, Mack could hear everything that went on in Molly's office. Well, not conversations but voice tones and types, and his door creaked every time the door to Molly's office opened.

And that was all the damn time.

Nobody gave her much of a break. Every half hour someone was knocking on her door, asking her a question, demanding something from her.

How did she get any work done?

Hell, he was next door and the constant traffic in and out of her room disturbed his work and broke his concentration...

Mack leaned back in his chair and eyed the many piles of paper on his desk, floor and on the small conference table in the corner. He could not believe that Jameson had let the paperwork run away with him. How did Jameson pay accurate sales and use tax, income tax? How did he know whether he was paying creditors accurately, whether his invoices matched the deliveries?

He now realized why Molly had been so reluctant to allow him to look at the paperwork; she knew it would deeply offend his anally retentive, need-control-at-all-costs soul. And he also knew she felt embarrassed, felt that it was her fault that the accounting system was in such a mess. Molly had an overdeveloped sense of responsibility; if any blame was to be laid, he'd drop it at Jameson's, and their useless bookkeeper's, door. From his observations, it seemed Beth liked to do as little work as possible, but still collect her large paycheck.

Jameson, bless him, was a brilliant host and exceptional at PR, but book work bored him. All his personal expenses were paid for by the business, and as long as there was a little money left in the bank account for some monogrammed shirts and fancy shoes, for him to buy an occasional antique or painting, and his damn Cuban cigars, he was happy.

Mack glared at the spreadsheet on his computer, conscious of the headache pounding behind his eyes, wishing he was looking at the color-coded, immaculate spreadsheets of his own business, able to pick up any information at a moment's notice.

He liked neat, he liked tidy and he liked control.

None of which he'd found here at Moonlight Ridge.

The books were a mess, and so was his head. He was crazy in lust with his ex-girlfriend, his one-time best friend, but she started work at seven and finished after six, sometimes seven at night. He suspected that if he wasn't in the picture, her working hours would be longer.

And that had to stop. Sure, he worked hard, but he made time for yoga, for exercise, for sex. His life, a long way from perfect, was a little more balanced than hers was.

Mack heard her door opening again, heard footsteps crossing the floor to her desk and heard low, rumbling masculine tones. It was the fourth time she'd been disturbed in twenty minutes and it was enough.

Mack understood that Molly adored Jameson, she felt guilty for stealing from him and was trying to redeem herself, but she was slowly, by degrees, killing herself.

That stopped. Right now.

Mack pushed back the leather chair, stood up and walked around his desk to the door connecting their offices. Not bothering to knock, he opened the door and two heads shot up to look at him. Molly frowned at him but Ross Barnes managed to flash him a smile. Mack replied to his greeting and walked to stand behind Molly, resting his shoulder against the wall.

He didn't speak but kept his eyes on Barnes, knowing that silence was an excellent way to demand an explanation. And while he waited, he reviewed what he knew about Ross. In his midthirties, he was Moonlight Ridge's catering and events manager and had years of experience in the field.

Since he'd heard his voice at least three times on separate occasions this morning, Mack had to wonder why, after years in the same position, he needed to speak to Molly so often.

He had many, many managers and he left them to get with their jobs and only interacted with them on a need-to-know basis.

"I was running some ideas by Molly for a fiftieth wedding anniversary party we are hosting in two weeks," Ross explained.

Mack's frown deepened. He'd seen the booking; it was a simple brunch for twenty people. Surely, someone with Ross's experience could handle that without Molly's input?

"You found it necessary to disturb Molly three times to discuss a minor event?" Mack asked, sounding skeptical.

"Uh—"

Molly turned around and nailed him with a hard look. "The mayor of Asheville will be attending. It might be a small brunch to you but it could lead to bigger functions."

No, the more likely explanation was that Moonlight Ridge's managers were, subtly and sneakily, delegating their work to Molly, using her loyalty and love of Jameson and the hotel to lighten their own loads.

Well, screw that. That stopped right now.

"I've been working next door and, by my account, Molly has had ten visitors in the last hour.

She has her own work to do and every interruption adds ten or fifteen minutes to the end of her day. You all work seven- to eight-hour days. Molly works a lot longer than that. It stops right now."

"Mack!"

Mack ignored Molly's furious expression.

"I want a meeting with all the heads of departments this afternoon at three. I will tell them the same thing. I think it's high time we instituted different protocols around here."

Barnes's mottled face reflected his anger and embarrassment. Mack didn't give a rat's ass; nobody was going to take advantage of Molly while he was around. And if he could reduce her stress and reduce her working hours, all the better.

"Jameson—"

Mack deepened his scowl and the rest of Barnes's sentence died on his lips. Good to know he wasn't losing his touch. He jerked his head toward the door and Barnes stood, rose and with a sour look at him, left Molly's office.

Molly spun around in her seat and looked up at him with her beautiful, intense, amazing eyes. In those clear depths he saw frustration, anger, and, was he imagining this, a little relief? Because there was no way Molly would take his high-handedness lying down.

Mack folded his arms, feeling defensive. "Before you cut me off at the knees, nobody gets to take advantage of you, Mol. Not Jameson, not your family and definitely not the staff. They are paid good salaries, have the experience and should be working independently of you."

Instead of lambasting him, as he expected, Molly just rested the back of her head on her leather chair and nodded. "I know. I should be tougher but I like being involved, I like knowing what's going on, feeling useful and being Jameson's eyes and ears."

Mack knew that for Molly, the hotel and Jameson represented stability and solidity, the one place and the one person that didn't change.

His father, for most of her life, had been her rock—and she felt she owed him—but that didn't mean she had to sacrifice her mental and physical health for him. And it was obvious that she was doing both.

What she needed was a break, some sun, to breathe fresh air. Grateful they weren't arguing, he pulled himself off the wall and held out his hands. "Let's go."

"Go where?" Molly asked, putting her hands in his and allowing him to pull her to her feet. Man, the woman was a feather. Along with working less, she needed to eat more.

He noticed the three dirty coffee mugs and shook his head. Too much work and way too much caffeine.

That, he decided, was going to change.

"Let's take a walk."

Molly nodded, reached for her cell and radio but Mack snatched them away before she could pick them up. Removing his phone from his pocket, he dumped all three devices in the top drawer of her desk and slammed it closed.

"I have to be available." Molly looked panicked, her corkscrew curls shaking.

"The world won't stop spinning if we take an hour off. Giada is with Jameson and everyone else can either find their own solution or wait until you return." Still holding her hands, Mack rested his forehead against hers. "Come walk with me, Mol, and let's check out for a little bit."

He saw the acquiescence in her eyes before he heard her small yes, saw her nod. Feeling like he'd both dodged a bullet and won the battle, Mack led her from her office, her hand warm and soft in his.

Eight

Her hand in his, Molly and Mack didn't speak as they walked down the long driveway toward the main road leading into Asheville. It felt strange not to have her phone in her pocket, her radio in her hand.

Strange but good.

The old cypress trees that lined either side of the driveway were showing off their bright new leaves and she could hear the brook chortling on its way to the lake. In the distance she could see two guests hiking up the steep hill to Tip's Point, a favorite walk of hers. From the lookout a few miles up the hill, they'd have an awesome view of the Blue Ridge Mountains.

She hadn't done that walk for ages, maybe a year. Two? Three? God, could it possibly be that long?

"You're frowning," Mack said, squeezing her hand. "You're supposed to be relaxing, not thinking."

Right. Molly tucked her free hand into the front pocket of her pants, conscious that her shoulders were up around her ears. She rolled them back, straightened her spine and made a mental note to find time for a deep massage.

But she knew she wouldn't; she hadn't visited the spa for an indulging treatment—waxing didn't count!—for many months. Possibly even a year or more.

Despite his high-handed manner on this subject, Mack did have a point. She allowed the staff to take advantage of her and she worked too hard.

But it was hard to change the habits of a lifetime. And she owed Jameson her loyalty and her effort—to work for her redemption. Without him, God knew where she'd be.

Mack nudged her shoulder, bringing her back to the present. "Just breathe and, for God's sake, stop thinking."

Molly sent him a wry look. That was easier said than done.

"Yeah, I know that's like asking for the moon but can you at least try?"

Stopping, Molly faced him. "Why are you doing this? Why do you care how stressed I am? Why are you trying to get me to relax?"

"Because you are wound tighter than a spinning top and you have no balance in your life."

"But why do you care?" Molly demanded. They'd had no contact for so long and it didn't make sense for him to slide back into his role as protective-in-chief. "I've been on my own for a long, long time, Mack, and I can take care of myself."

Mack lifted his hand to squeeze her left trapezius muscle. His fingers encountered a rock-solid wall and she pulled away from the pain. "You're stressed to the max, Molly, and, while I'm here and have some sort of power, I *will* make life easier for you. It's BS that you work such long hours and that you juggle a hundred balls, ninety of which don't even belong to you."

Underneath his designer clothing, expensive cologne and the urbane mask was still the boy who would move heaven and earth for her. It was both wonderful and terrifying.

Mack, she had to remember, had left her, breaking her heart and her spirit. She would not allow that to happen again.

They were temporary colleagues, temporary friends having a temporary fling. End of story.

Mack placed his hand on her back, steering her down the road toward a rambling stone structure. The barn, standing to the side of the road, was empty, its roof still intact. It was part of the history of the farm and an interesting feature and while it was pretty, it wasn't useful.

"I've tried to talk to Jameson about knocking it down but he won't hear of it," Molly told Mack.

Mack walked down the overgrown driveway and stepped up to the front door, warped by the weather. "He promised Tip he'd never pull it down because it was built before the main house."

Tip O'Sullivan's parents, professional socialites, built the house a century ago. They added one wing to accommodate their incessant stream of guests and within a few years converted the estate into a hotel and resort. Tip added on another wing and Jameson built the pretty lakeside cottages to accommodate more guests.

Yet, in all that time, this stone barn stood untouched on a rise overlooking the lake.

Molly watched as Mack put his shoulder to the door and pushed. The door opened with a loud complaint and Mack stood back and gestured her to precede him.

"After you," Mack said.

Molly heard the tremble in his voice and swallowed her huge grin. "No, please, after you," she insisted.

Mack glared at her. "Hah, funny. Get in there and do your thing."

It was a long-held agreement between them that Mack would deal with all critters they found on their adventures—from frogs to snakes to bugs—but she was the person in charge of exterminating spiders.

Mack loathed spiders and it seemed nothing had changed. Before he would step into the barn, she'd have to do a recce and tell him, exactly, how many spiders she could see and where they were. Mack, tall and broad and tough as hell, was deathly scared of arachnids.

"Wuss," Molly said, brushing past him. Stepping into the empty structure, she placed her hands on her hips, looking at the stone walls, the exposed timbers of the roof and the way the sunlight streamed through the windows on the side of the building looking out to the lake. It was a stunning spot and Molly thought it would be lovely if it was converted into a private, self-catering villa.

But the conversion would cost a bomb, or two, and the business didn't have the credit or cash flow to support that sort of expansion. And, since they had too many rooms open too often, she couldn't justify any expensive renovations.

"Spiders, Mol," Mack reminded her, still standing just outside the door.

Molly did a cursory look around, didn't see any spiders and gestured for him to come in. Mack did his own quick sweep and he gradually relaxed.

Coming to stand next to her, he whistled as he took in the huge space and the lovely light. "Wow, it's amazing."

Molly trailed her hand down a stone wall, wondering who built this place so long ago. "Isn't it? I was just thinking that it would be awesome as a private villa. With clever renovations it could sleep six or eight." She gestured through the broken windowpane to the clear lake. Two guests were idly rowing across the lake, their faces tipped to the sun.

Molly caught the quick shake of his head and sighed. "I know. Until we fill up every room every night, I can't think about converting anything."

"It would be a really good idea…if we had the guests," Mack replied.

Molly darted a look at him. "Can I run something by you?"

"You know you can."

"I'm standing by all the ideas in my proposal because they are necessary."

Mack gestured for her to carry on talking.

"But I'm thinking that we should make Moonlight Ridge even more exclusive, more difficult to get into. I think we should hike the prices, reduce the numbers and turn it into a boutique hotel, a place people should be fighting, and definitely waiting, to get into."

Her desire to run an exquisite, exclusive place, providing her guests with the best of the best, burned in her soul. This was the way to go, she was certain of it. But would Mack agree?

Mack thought for a moment. "I think it's a great idea, I do. But we still need to get people here, a reason why they'd choose Moonlight Ridge over a hundred others," Mack pointed out.

"If only Travis would come back and open a world-class restaurant here. That would bring the guests in. I've heard that his Traverser restaurants are booked up for months and months in advance," Molly said.

"Yep, they are. Travis is a fabulous chef and he's making a name for himself in the haute cuisine world."

Molly heard the pride in his voice and hid her smile. The brothers' relationship might be strained but it wasn't completely broken. She was glad for Mack; family was important and she hoped that Mack, Grey and Travis found their way back to one another. Back in the day, they'd been a tight-as-hell team.

"All of his restaurants are in great cities— Atlanta, LA, London. Asheville is hip and trendy but I don't know if it's sophisticated enough for a Traverser," Mack stated, his brow furrowed.

Damn.

"But you're right. An excellent restaurant could bring guests to Moonlight Ridge."

Molly watched as Mack paced the room and saw the intense look of speculation on his face. His face held the same expression it did when he was ten and contemplating building a ramp for his BMX bike, plans for the treehouse, how to raise enough money to buy the F-150 truck he'd been eyeing since he was twelve.

Mack had hit on a plan; of that Molly was certain.

Mack paced out the width of the barn, then the length, coming back to stand in the middle of the room, his expression thoughtful.

"Are you going to share what's going on in that big brain of yours?" Molly asked, leaning her back against the stone wall and lifting her booted foot to rest its sole on the wall.

Mack turned around to face her. "Actually, I was thinking this would be a perfect spot for a Corkscrew Craft Beer brewery."

"I never understood why you chose that name." Molly wrinkled her nose. "I mean, a person associates corkscrews with wine bottles, not craft beer."

When he looked at her, his face was inscrutable. "It has nothing to do with wine or corkscrews."

"Then I really don't understand."

Mack took two steps, lifted a strand of her hair and wound it around his index finger, watching as the curl hugged his finger. "Corkscrew curls, Mol. I've always loved your hair."

Molly sucked in her breath, completely blind-sided by his admission. He'd named his company after her? What the hell? Why? "I don't understand why you would do that."

Mack dropped his hand and turned away. Ignoring her silent plea for an explanation, he pointed to the back wall, where there were no windows. "I'd add on space at the back, for the processing and distribution of the beer, but I'd put the tanks there where the diners could see them. In front of them, a really long statement bar. A small, open kitchen in the corner, and we'd have a small, beer-inspired menu. I'd go for an industrial look inside, to contrast with the wooden beams and the stone walls. Heavy tables, a concrete floor. I'd leave the stonework exposed. Maybe we could open up that far wall, make a deck and put tables out there, too. The customers would enjoy the view."

Forcing herself not to grab his shirt and demand why he felt the need to name his company after her hair—her hair, for goodness' sake!—Molly struggled to think. It wasn't easy when she wanted to beat an answer out of him.

Pulling up her business brain took far more effort than she expected.

"And how, exactly, would your brewery benefit the resort?"

Mack took a moment to digest her question, his thoughts obviously a million miles away. "Well, I'd have to buy the building, giving Jameson an immediate and rather substantial cash injection."

Which would be lovely but she needed more than cash; she needed guests, as she'd told him.

"I don't own and run Traverser-like restaurants but actually, people do travel to visit my breweries. I have no doubt that some people would choose to stay at Moonlight Ridge. Some would stay over, visit the spa, want to take a hike… maybe we could do joint promotions between Moonlight Ridge and the brewery. The point is, we want to up the visibility of the resort, and the brewery would be a good way to do it."

Molly wrinkled her nose. "Aren't we looking at two different segments of the market? The resort caters to the very rich while the brewery is more middle-of-the-road, isn't it?"

Amusement flashed across Mack's face. "Actually, you would be surprised at the demographics of who visits my breweries. According to the expensive company I recently hired to do consumer research, the young and wealthy account for at least half of my customer base. And isn't that the segment of the market you are looking at attracting?"

He had her there. "Fair point."

Mack looked around the space again and Molly could see his mind working at warp speed. "I'd need an architect to help me plan the space."

Molly had spent too much time taking virtual tours of his many breweries on the Corkscrew Breweries website—and really, every time she remembered that he'd named his business after her hair, her heart did a strange triple thump—and all his places carried the same subtle branding and design elements.

He'd call in his usual design team and within months the brewery would be up and running. When Mack wanted something, he didn't let anything get in his way.

"I need to talk to Jameson and if he agrees,

I'll get my senior management team out here to do some market research and viability studies. Asheville has many craft breweries but my gut says mine will be a welcome addition. But I'd like the research to confirm my hunch. Once we make the final decision, I'll get Vanna out here to inspect the building, to start working on some design plans."

"Is she an architect?"

"Yeah, she's worked on most of my breweries," Mack responded, his thoughts miles away.

Molly knew that she was wandering into a minefield but they couldn't keep avoiding the subject forever. "Why did you never ask Grey to do any work for you? I mean, he is one of the most in-demand, award-winning architects around."

Guilt and annoyance replaced excitement. "I try to keep family and work separate."

Molly rolled her eyes and made sure he saw her dramatic gesture. "Thousands might believe you. I don't."

"Drop it, Mol," Mack growled.

That wasn't going to happen. "Why are you three still not talking? It's ridiculous, Mack!"

Mack made a show of looking around the

empty, decrepit building. "How did we go from talking about this barn to my family?" he asked, his tone suggesting that she back down.

She never had and never would.

"Why aren't you and your brothers talking, Mack?" Molly persisted.

Mack started to walk away but Molly placed her hand on his roped-with-muscle forearm. She ignored the flash of heat and the corresponding lust. This was more important than the still-bubbling desire.

"I confided in you, Mack."

She had him there and he knew it.

"We do talk."

That was such a lie. "I'm not talking about quick conversations about Jameson and you know it. You guys were tight, best friends as well as brothers, but now you are little more than strangers."

"Yeah, well, nearly killing them in a car crash tends to change the dynamic," Mack muttered, grief and regret coating the bitter words.

Had he spent the past fifteen years blaming himself? Surely not? Molly chose her next words carefully. "Mack, it was an accident. Everyone knows that."

When his eyes met hers Molly saw, for the first time, the guilt lodged deep in his soul.

"I lost control, Molly, and the blame is mine to shoulder. I was behind the wheel. I put that truck into the ditch."

"I was told you were all arguing, that you were distracted," Molly protested.

Mack's expression turned hard and she could feel him pulling back, creating distance between them. "I am the oldest—"

"By months, for God's sake!"

Mack ignored her interruption. "—and I was responsible for looking after them, for their safety. I failed and Travis nearly died. I lost my right to a family because I failed to look after them. I allowed myself to be distracted, to lose control and *it will never happen again.*"

Wow. Mack had always been hard on himself but this was ridiculous. "You are being insanely tough on yourself."

"No, I'm really not."

Molly frowned, hearing the subtext beneath that hard statement. "What aren't you telling me?"

"Leave it alone, Molly." Mack turned to walk toward the door but Molly ran to stand between him and the door, stretching her arms out wide to create a barrier between him and the exit.

Mack sent her a "get real" look. "Molly, I'm bigger and stronger than you and could just lift you up and out of my way."

Molly dropped her arms. "Yeah, of course you could." Her eyes clashed with his and she sighed at all the pain in those deep, dark depths. "Tell me, Mack."

She wanted to know; the curiosity was killing her. But more important, she sensed that, like her theft, this was a piece of the past that needed to see the light.

"My mom died at childbirth."

She knew that. He'd been raised by his dad until he was seven. One day, his father dropped him off at school and never bothered to collect him. Mack never heard from him again.

"I know, Mack," Molly replied, keeping her tone gentle and nonconfrontational.

"But I never told you it was my fault she died."

He didn't have to; it was never the baby's fault when a mother died. But instead of telling him that, she just tipped her head to the side and waited for more.

"I was a big baby, and she was tiny. I was two

or three weeks late and they induced her. Officially, the cause of death was post-partum bleeding from an obstructed labor."

"That sounds reasonable and none of it your fault," Molly said.

"That's not what my father told me every single day of my life," Mack whispered, his hands clenched at his sides.

Oh, God. Molly muttered a silent string of curse words before stepping forward to place her hand on his chest, directly above his heart, needing the connection. "You know that's rubbish, Mack."

Mack raised his shoulders halfway to his ears before allowing them to drop. "Intellectually, I do. Emotionally, not so much. And the things you are told as a young kid tend to stick with you."

Mack raked his hand through his dark hair and Molly noticed the slight tremble in his fingers. "He told me that I should've died, not her."

And she didn't need to be a rocket scientist to know that he thought that he should've been injured, not Travis. "Oh, Mack, you know it doesn't work like that. It wasn't your fault."

Mack stared at a point past her shoulder, his

body tight with tension. "After I came to live with Jameson, I was terrified of messing up, of doing anything wrong. I was the model kid. Jameson said jump and I leaped. I didn't want to give him an excuse to give me back."

She didn't know any of this; maybe they hadn't been as close as they thought they were. Then again, they'd been kids and Mack had never been one to wear his heart on his sleeve.

"When Grey and Travis arrived, I started to relax a little because they were far worse behaved than I was and Jameson never sent them away, or even threatened to."

Man, what had it felt like to live with so much insecurity? Molly knew how much she worried about Jameson ever finding out about the money she stole, how it would change their relationship, and it kept her awake at night. She'd been a young adult but Mack had lived with his guilt a lot longer than she had. And it wasn't his fault!

God, if she could she'd hunt down his father and slap him stupid. What a bastard!

"The accident just reminded me that it's better for people if I keep my distance, if I stay away."

Molly stared at him and shook her head. Then she lifted her hand and smacked it back down on his chest, the sound jerking his eyes back to her face. Gripping his shirt, she looked up into his anguished eyes and tried to shake him. Because he was so much bigger than she was, she didn't move him an inch.

"All right, *enough*. Seriously, Mack, you're done with thinking like that. It was not your fault your mother died and your father had no right to blame you! Her death was horrible, but it was not your fault!"

She caught a flicker of hope in his eyes that was quickly extinguished. She tapped his chest again, trying to make her point. "*It. Was. Not. Your. Fault.* Are we clear on that?"

Mack kept his eyes on hers, his hands coming up to rest on her waist. Well, at least he was listening to her, and was she imagining the fact that some of the tension in his body had dissipated?

"As for the car accident, I know that you were all arguing and, hell, Mack, you know how heated your arguments could be. I was witness to so many of your fights back then. Testosterone was raging, you all wanted to be right and God, you were all as stubborn as each other. I can easily imagine the argument in the truck and I'm not surprised you got distracted. It's a horrible curve, it was dark and raining and you were all yelling at each other. You were *all* stupid, *all* irresponsible and if there is blame to be assigned, it should be shared. But you were kids and it was an accident, for God's sake."

Mack shook his head. "I was driving—"

Molly stepped back and folded her arms across her chest. "I can't change your mind about how you feel about the past, Mack. Only you can. All I can tell you is that your father's stupid words and an accident a long time ago shouldn't still have so much power."

"But it does," Mack told her, his words coated with sorrow and grief.

Molly rested her hand on his cheek, feeling the stubble under her hand, the hard line of his jaw. "Only you can change that, Mack. Not me, not Jameson, not your brothers. Only you."

It would be easy to change the subject, to brush aside the emotion and flit onto another subject, but Molly liked Mack too much—more than she should—to allow that to happen. She stepped closer to him and wrapped her arms around his trim waist, hoping to hug away the desolate look on his face.

Unlike her, Mack had nothing to be ashamed of.

Mack didn't say much on their walk back to Moonlight Ridge and when they reached the third floor, he disappeared into his office without a word. Knowing that she needed to give him space, Molly immersed herself in her own work. When she finally stopped, somewhere around seven, she noticed that the light was off in his office.

She returned back to her apartment, saw that the guesthouse was in darkness and assumed Mack was with Jameson. She cooked, ate, drank a glass of wine and wondered whether Mack would come to her tonight.

And she kept wondering for another hour, then two. At half past ten, minutes before she was about to give up on him and go to bed, she saw the lights come on in the guesthouse and she debated whether to go to him or to give him space.

But like her, Mack tended to spend too much time in his head, and she knew of a truly excellent way of getting him to step outside his big brain. It involved getting naked and Molly knew Mack had no problem with that...

Minutes later Molly found herself standing at his closed door and lifted her hand to knock. But before her hand could make contact with the wood, the door opened and Mack stood there, looking at her like she was wholly unexpected.

"Ah, you're here."

"I am."

Mack rubbed his jaw, then pushed his hand through his hair. "I was just coming to you," he said, not sounding very enthusiastic. "Just so you know, I'm not in the mood to talk."

Ah. He assumed she'd come over here to revive their earlier conversation.

"Well, if you don't want to talk, what would you prefer to do? Play Monopoly? Drink wine? Cheat at poker?" she teased him.

"Strip poker, maybe," Mack growled, tugging her into the hallway. Placing his hot mouth on her bare neck, he shuddered. He lifted his head to speak again. "I just need to lose myself in you, Curls."

"I think I can make that happen," Molly told him, her lips curving.

Mack, not wasting any time, immediately

pulled her dress up the back of her thighs and palmed her butt with his broad hand. He pushed his other hand into her hair, gripping her head and angling her face to receive his demanding, possessive kiss. Tongues dueled as he explored her mouth, rediscovering her, learning about the woman she was today.

It was enthralling to be the object of so much focused passion and the reason for his brief, husky statements of appreciation. Needing to feel him, Molly pulled his shirt up so that she could touch his hot body. Her fingers traced the rows of his six-pack and the long muscles that covered his hips, before drifting over the hard erection that tented his jeans.

Ooh, very nice. She traced his long length with the tip of her finger. And, because she could, did it again.

"Love that, baby," Mack muttered, bunching her dress up to her hips, revealing her white bikini panties. Annoyed with the barrier, he pulled the dress up and over her head and dropped it to the floor. Resting his forehead against hers, he looked down her body, past her flat stomach to her long legs. She was still in her heels.

"Ah, Mol. You…this…" He shuddered. "You in my arms is everything, and more, than I imagined."

"Is that a good or a bad thing?" Molly asked as her bra fell to the floor.

"It's a very excellent thing, Curls."

Mack slid his hand between her legs and cupped her, his thumb immediately finding and brushing her sensitive bundle of nerves. She released a soft yelp and immediately wanted more.

"Mack, I need you," Molly moaned against his lips, lifting her hips to push herself against his shaft.

Mack's hand stilled and his breath against her nipple was fire hot. "If we don't slow down, I'm going to take you right here, right now."

"So do it," Molly challenged him, tipping her head back to connect with his deeply dark and passion-soaked eyes.

"Good thing I came prepared." Mack smiled and pulled a strip of condoms from the back pocket of his jeans. He ripped a packet off with his teeth and allowed the rest to drop to the floor. He pressed the condom into her hand.

As Mack pulled off his shirt, Molly opened

the first button of his jeans, then the second, and when they were loose around his hips she shoved her hands inside his briefs and pushed both underwear and jeans down his hips. His erection stood tall and proud, and Molly sighed at how big he was...

She couldn't wait for him to be inside her. She wanted to be filled, stretched, taken to the limit. She wanted him...

Molly pulled out the condom and swiftly rolled it over his erection, sucking in her breath as he hardened even further. Mack released a soft curse before hooking his hands under her thighs and lifting her, spreading her legs to either side of his waist. The head of his penis pushed against her wet, warm core.

Mack pressed her against the front door and pinned her there with his body, sliding into her with one long, confident, sexy stroke. Her world narrowed, everything faded away and there were only Mack's hands on her thighs, his tongue in her mouth mimicking the thrust of his hips, the hot strokes inside her as he pushed her higher and higher.

She whimpered, stretching for that ultimate

release, wanting to step inside pleasure, to become pleasure.

Mack dropped his head to murmur encouragement in her ear. "You are so damn sexy, baby. I can't wait to feel you come on me, around me."

"Mack!" Molly yelled, reaching for her release.

Molly shouted as stars exploded behind her eyeballs and her body splintered into a million pieces. She vaguely heard Mack's yell in her ear, felt him shudder as he fell apart, his fingers digging into her hips.

Mack pushed into her and connected with something deep inside. She flew again, pleasure fueling her flight. She screamed his name again before fracturing once more.

Molly had no idea how much time passed when she returned to earth, her face in his neck, still pinned to the door by his hard body.

"I don't think we did that properly, Mol. I think we might have to do that again." She heard Mack's laughter in his words, felt the curve of his lips against her temple. "And again, until we get it right."

The problem was that she thought it might take the rest of their lives to get it *exactly* right. And, even more scary, she was game to try.

Nine

Mack stared at the spreadsheet he'd spent the past few weeks working on, the numbers dancing in front of his eyes. He pushed his thumb and index finger into his eyeballs, hoping to ease the burn.

Dropping his hands, he stared at the total at the bottom on his column and cursed violently, the words bouncing off the walls of the office. The total was still the same and he knew it would never change.

Before he could second-guess himself, he opened his browser and did a large file transfer, sending a copious amount of scanned documents and spreadsheets to Grey's email address, hoping his brother would find a reasonable explanation for what he'd discovered.

Mack spun around in his chair and stared out the window behind his desk, into the dark shadows of Moonlight Ridge's extensive gardens below. In the distance he could see the yellow lights of one occupied cottage on the edge of the lake but otherwise, the grounds were in darkness.

Mack looked at his watch, saw that it was nearly eleven and thought of Molly, curled up in his bed in the guesthouse, hopefully fast asleep. They'd been sleeping together for the past six weeks and, strangely, he still hadn't tired of her. Usually, by this point in a relationship he'd be looking for an easy exit, concocting a strategy to slide out of his lover's life.

Truthfully, he couldn't remember when, if ever, he had a fling that lasted this long. Ironic that his two longest relationships were with the same woman.

Mack turned back to his screen and frowned, wishing he could avoid having to tell her what had taken him weeks to discover. With her history, Molly would take it personally, would blame herself for what had happened.

She needed to know as quickly as possible, but before he told her, he needed to tell his brothers so Mack picked up his phone and shot off a text to them, asking if they were able to talk.

Grey replied immediately, saying he was free but Travis's message went unanswered for a couple of minutes. When he did reply, he said that he was in the middle of service and couldn't talk right now.

After telling Travis to call him when he was free, Mack started a video call to Grey and within a minute his brother's face appeared on his monitor, blue eyes wary. God, he was so sick of seeing the distance, the cool composure on his siblings' faces.

He wanted his brothers back. They needed to talk, to discuss that night so long ago, to, if they could, put it behind them. He missed them, intensely. Horribly. Being back in Asheville, living and breathing the air and atmosphere of Moonlight Ridge, made him realize that they'd wasted so much damn time.

He wanted his family back...

Grey's question broke into his thoughts. "Mack, what's up?"

It wasn't the time or the place for a heal-the-past type of conversation; he'd prefer to speak to his brothers in person, to apologize to their faces and not to a screen. And he would apologize and ask for their forgiveness. He hoped, prayed, he got it.

"Mack?"

Mack met his brother's eyes. "Hey, thanks for taking my call." So formal, so stiff. That had to change. And soon, dammit. "I hope I'm not interrupting anything important."

The corners of Grey's mouth lifted, somehow knowing that Mack was referring to a date or sex. "I'm in my office, at my desk, working."

"Busy?" Mack asked, hoping Grey wouldn't shut him down.

"Yeah, always," Grey replied, looking a little surprised at his question. He didn't blame him since they only ever discussed Moonlight Ridge or Jameson.

Mack rubbed the back of his neck, wanting to delay telling Grey the bad news. Instead, he decided to broach an idea he'd been considering. "Do you remember the old barn at the bottom of the property?" It was a stupid question; of course Grey would remember the barn. It had only stood there all their lives.

"Sure," Grey replied.

"I spoke to Jameson and I'm thinking about repurposing it, establishing one of my breweries there. What do you think?"

Grey thought for a minute before smiling. "I think it's a great idea. It needs to be used, to be lived in again."

"It's a great space but it needs to be reworked." Mack sucked in a deep breath, annoyed to realize that he was nervous. "I need an architect. You interested?"

Grey's eyes widened, and astonishment jumped into them and fluttered across his face. "You want me to bid for the job?"

"No, I want *you* to design my new brewery. I don't care what you charge. I just want my brother to work on this project with me."

Grey's astonishment didn't fade. "It's been a while since you've called me your brother, Mack," he quietly stated, sounding bemused.

Mack rubbed the back of his neck again, feeling his skin prickling. "Yeah, I know. Look, we need to talk but I'm done with this cold war. Can we talk sometime, about you working with me on the brewery?" He hesitated before deciding to dive in. "I also want to talk about the accident, to find a way to move forward?"

Was that relief he saw in Grey's eyes or was he imagining it? Grey nodded. "Yeah, I think that's a good idea. Let's talk, Mack."

"I'd like to get the renovations to the barn done as soon as possible but I will wait for a gap in your schedule," Mack told him, feeling a warm wave of relief sliding through him.

"I could work on the design when I take over from you at the end of the month," Grey told him. "It's going to be a real pain moving back to Moonlight Ridge but I promised to do it."

"When you get here, listen to Molly. I mean, *really* listen to her and support her ideas. No one knows the resort better than she does, and her ideas will put Moonlight Ridge back on the map."

Grey looked amused at his words and Mack saw the he's-getting-lucky thought cross his mind.

Mack ignored Grey's curious expression and thought about going back to Nashville, resuming his normal routine, and his stomach clenched. The life he knew two months ago no longer seemed normal; waking up with Molly seemed right; sharing a carafe of coffee on the porch seemed normal; chatting with her throughout the day was what he wanted to do. But he did need to check on his brewery in Austin and to investigate why his Santa Fe operation was experiencing a huge dip in turnover. He had to go back to work. But he didn't, necessarily, want to return to Nashville.

Asheville, dammit, was starting to feel like home again. That wasn't what he expected when he made the long drive from Nashville weeks ago.

Grey asked Mack how Jameson was and they passed a couple of minutes discussing Jameson's health. Mack told him that Jameson fired Giada every other day but his nurse simply ignored their father's fiery declarations. Giada was also refusing access to his cigars, another battle in an on-going war.

They both agreed that Giada was tougher than she looked and could handle their grumpy, stubborn father.

"Dad wants us home for a Sunday lunch like we used to have," Grey told him.

"I heard," Mack replied. "I'd like that, actually."

"I would, too. But is there any chance his cooking has improved?"

Mack smiled at Grey's grimace. Jameson loved Sunday lunches and insisted on cooking for his family. Unfortunately, they were always a disaster with burnt duck, undercooked potatoes and overcooked vegetables. Sunday lunches, and Henri, the resort's previous chef, were the reason Travis started cooking and launched his love affair with food.

"Maybe we can persuade Travis to cook," Grey mused, "if we can get him home."

"We both know Trav will find a way to get out of it," Mack quietly stated.

Grey nodded. "Admittedly, with his insane work schedule, we were damn lucky to get his commitment to do a look-after-Moonlight Ridge shift after me. He won't come back before he has to."

Of the three of them, Travis was, by a hair's breadth, the most stubborn. If, and when, the three of them got together next, he'd find a way to get through to his stubborn-ass baby brother. He was tired of living his life without them in it.

Grey gestured to his desk. "I've still got a few hours' work ahead of me, M. Send me the dimensions and any ideas you have on the barn and I'll mull over some ideas of my own."

"Sounds good," Mack said before grimacing. "But actually, that wasn't why I called you, Grey."

Grey's eyes sharpened. "Then why did you call me?"

"I've just emailed you a lot of paperwork, including accounts, payments and reports. You've always been great at numbers and I need a second opinion. I hope I'm wrong, but I think someone is stealing from Moonlight Ridge."

Grey returned his call an hour later and this time Travis was able to join their three-way video call.

"So I hate to confirm your suspicions, Mack, but yeah, from what I can see, money has been taken from Moonlight Ridge."

Mack winced, wishing that he'd been wrong. This was going to kill Molly.

Mack gripped the bridge of his nose with his finger and thumb. "Are you sure?"

Grey nodded. "Yeah. Look, I did a cursory look at the material you sent through but I picked up quite a few instances of double dipping—"

"What the hell is double dipping?" Travis asked.

"Basically, the thief submits a claim for an expense on a credit card and gets reimbursed. Later, she—he—submits a cash reimbursement request for the same expense. Double dipping," Grey explained.

"Okay." Travis rubbed the back of his neck. "And how long has this been happening?"

Grey shrugged. "At a guess? Years and years. Jameson also made it easy for the thief to operate because, by God, I have never seen such a crazy accounting system in my life."

Neither had Mack.

"Talking about our father, are we going to tell him about this?" Grey asked.

"Hell, no. He's not supposed to be stressed, remember?" Mack snapped. Hearing that there was another thief at Moonlight Ridge would cause Jameson to stop convalescing and start bashing heads together.

Mack looked at his computer monitor. On the left side was Grey's face, on the right Travis's.

"I agree," Travis said, his deep baritone a lot like Jameson's. Despite them not sharing any DNA, Travis and Jameson had the same deep voice and the same build, and Travis learned how to be tenacious and stubborn from watching their father.

They all had.

He was so sick at being at odds with his brothers, Mack thought. Tired of wasting time, seeing another week, another month, go past without them connecting.

He'd reconnected with Molly and he now knew how great that felt. He wanted more of it, wanted his family whole and happy again.

Even if it meant eating Jameson's terrible food, he wanted those Sunday family lunches, Molly at his side, his hand on her thigh under the table.

He could see it, almost taste it. Jameson sitting at the head of the table, refusing to allow anyone else to carve the duck. The table would be piled high with dishes; Grey and Travis would be arguing about something because, hell, that was what they did. But it would be a friendly argument, a lot of teasing and trash-talking. He didn't know whom his brothers would end up with, not yet, but he could sense their women at the table, laughing and drinking wine together, discussing clothes and babies and art and politics.

Smart women, fun women.

And his hand would be on the thigh of the

smartest, loveliest woman he'd ever met. The only female who'd ever touched his soul.

His first love and his last love.

The feeling that he only ever wanted to be where Molly was had been steadily enveloping him the past few weeks. And if Molly wanted to be here, then he had to consider making some changes including moving his company head-quarters to Asheville. If he wanted to be with Molly, and God, he did, then that was the only course of action that made sense. He'd still travel but maybe he could buy a small piece of land be-hind the pond, build a house for him and Molly, and their kids, to share. He'd travel for work but he'd always come home to Moonlight Ridge, to Molly.

If she'd have him…

"We need a forensic accountant to dig deeper, to do proper accounting," Grey suggested.

Mack pulled his attention back to the prob-lem at hand. "I presume it will take some time to get a forensic accountant in place. So what can Molly and I do to try and find out who is the embezzler in the meantime?" Mack asked.

The look on Grey's face had his heart plummet-ing to his toes. "That's not a good idea, Mack."

"Why not?" Mack asked, though a part of him knew what was coming.

"Molly is in charge of the company credit cards and it's her signature on some of the claim requests."

Ah, hell, no.

"I'm grateful that I'm on the other side of the screen and you can't hit me as I ask this…" Grey grimaced, hesitating. "But are you sure it isn't Molly who is the embezzler, Mack? From the reports you sent me, she looks like the most likely person to have done this."

Mack swallowed down his instinctive response, which was to rip Grey's head off for the suggestion. Mack ground his back teeth together and forced the words out. "Of course it's not Molly, Grey. Despite what it looks like."

A cold fist slammed into his sternum, expelling his warm and fuzzy feelings. Was he wrong to instinctively defend her? Was he blinded by lust, by memories, by their shared history? Was he looking for a reason to absolve her because he didn't *want* her to be guilty?

But dammit, because of her confession, there was a tiny flicker of doubt.

Mack forced himself to think, to be the cool-headed, rational, thinking person he normally was. If this was anyone else but Molly, how would he respond to Grey's statement?

With skepticism and doubt and with a burning desire to know, one way or the other. Guilt rolled over him, hot and sour. Mack felt the pull between blind faith and loyalty and his own innate suspicion and cynicism. After all, she had stolen from Jameson before...

Guilt crashed over him and he was glad he was sitting down.

"It's not Molly," he stated, wondering if he was trying to convince himself or his brothers.

"How do you know that, Mack?" Travis asked. "It's been a long time since she was part of your life and you don't know her anymore."

Oh, yes, he did. But doubt, insidious and relentless, mocked his loyalty. "It's *not* Molly."

Did his brothers hear the note of hesitation in his voice? Because he sure as hell did.

"I'd like to believe that," Grey replied, his voice steady. "I've always liked Molly but it would be nice to have some proof."

"What happened to innocent until proven guilty?" Mack demanded. His hesitancy about her integrity would be something he kept to himself. *Always.*

"It's a nice concept but this is real life, Mack. If this gets out, and it will, it will become news. Jameson is hugely popular in Asheville and the press loves him. They will go nuts when they discover that there's another thief at Moonlight Ridge and that the chief suspect is his protégé and the daughter of the man who embezzled from him before. And we all know that bad publicity is the last thing Moonlight Ridge needs."

Mack looked at Travis. "What do you think, Travis?"

Travis nodded. "I agree with Grey. It's been a long time and the Molly we knew could be long gone."

Mack ran a hand over his face, feeling sick to his stomach. They had, dammit to hell and back, a point. If Molly were any other employee at Moonlight Ridge, they'd put that person on a leave of absence until they could get to the bottom of the mess.

It would take a lot of time, effort and knowledge, forensic accounting knowledge, to find some solid proof, and that leave of absence could be weeks or months. If he did that to her, Molly's reputation would take a hell of a hit. If she was innocent, she'd feel betrayed and mentally eviscerated. And she'd never forgive him…

His rational, business brain—the part of him that looked at the world without emotion—accepted that his brothers had a point. His intuition, his soul, dammit, was screaming at him to trust Molly, to remember what she told him about why she stole from Jameson before, reminding him how gutted and guilty she felt for her actions as a young adult.

Beth could be the thief; after all, it wasn't a big jump from blackmail to theft. She was bright enough to make it look like Molly was the thief…but then Mack remembered that Beth hadn't been at Moonlight Ridge that long and the pilfering had been going on for years. Not Beth then. Damn.

Could it be Molly? Was she playing him? She'd taken money before; she could do it again, if the stakes were high enough. Her reasons would be good; it wouldn't be for her personal gain. Had her brothers got into some sort of debt they couldn't repay? Was her mom sick? Was she still paying off her student loans…?

No, none of that felt right. Or was he just wanting her to be innocent? Molly was trustworthy, he was sure of it. But what if he was wrong and she wasn't?

What then?

Molly ran up the back stairs to her office, feeling light and a little lovely on this bright, early-summer morning. She'd heard Mack rolling out of bed, felt his kiss on her cheek, his murmured instruction for her to sleep in. Happy to listen, she'd rolled over and slid into a deep sleep, the best she'd had for months, maybe years.

Mack returned home extremely late last night and she'd woken to his mouth on the ball of her shoulder, his hand between her legs. She'd tried to talk to him but he'd told her to hush and slowly, thoroughly made love to her. Time and time again she fell apart in his arms. No wonder she'd slept like the dead.

There was magic between them and being together made sense.

It always had.

Molly stopped on the landing, placed her hand against the wall, remembering the first time she felt this sense of "rightness." She'd been eight and Mack reattached the head of her favorite

Barbie Grant decapitated in a fit of rage. There were a thousand little moments from then on—him helping her with math, looking down into the front row from the stage to see his eyes on her, the first time they made love—and, hopefully, there would be tens of thousands of those moments in their future.

She was his and he was hers; they'd always each been one half of a whole.

Maybe it was time to stop fighting that...

Mack loved her, of that she was certain. He knew her and, when she confessed her sins, he'd chosen to believe the best of her, not the worst. It would've been so easy for him to judge her actions and paint her with the same brush as her dad, but he'd dug deeper, peeling back the surface to discover her motivations.

And maybe, with his understanding and forgiveness, she could, sometime soon, forgive herself and accept that she'd been pushed into a horrible position; a child who'd felt alone and abandoned.

In showing her compassion, Mack taught her to be compassionate to herself.

As soon as Jameson was stronger, she'd have a chat with him, confess her sins and let go of the guilt. She'd hand him a check, plus interest, and he'd, hopefully, be as understanding as Mack. Jameson, burly, big and gruff, had taught his sons tolerance so Molly was hopeful that everything would be okay.

Oh, she had no idea what the future held, how she and Mack would make this work going forward. Or even if they could. In a few short weeks, he'd be back in Nashville, and then he'd be back on the road, whipping around the country to check on his businesses. Molly was under no illusions that they'd have a traditional relationship, or that a white wedding or 2.4 kids were in her future.

She could drive herself crazy trying to figure out the future. The past was behind her, the future was unknown so all she could do was to give this moment, today, her entire attention.

And yes, let's be honest here, after being thoroughly loved last night, today she was feeling pretty damn fine.

Molly walked into her office, dumped her laptop bag on her desk, grimaced at the folders she saw there and resisted the urge to walk into Mack's office and try and talk him into playing hooky with her today. They could hike up to Tip's Point, make love in the back meadow nobody knew about. Or they could try out the new east-meets-west fusion restaurant in downtown Asheville.

They could drink wine, take some time...

But hell, it was the end of the month and they'd taken most of yesterday off. Mack not only needed time to do whatever month's-end duties he had for his own company, but he had payroll checks to sign for Moonlight Ridge, supplier payments to authorize and, as he'd mentioned, a series of online meetings scheduled.

And she had her own work to do...lots of it.

Being responsible was such a pain in the ass.

Molly stood in the doorway of the door that connected their offices and took a moment to study Mack, whose attention was on his monitor, fingers flying across his keyboard. A pair of black-rimmed reading glasses sat on his nose and he looked like a sexy scientist or a hot accountant.

And Molly fell in love, once again. At the rate she was going, by the time Mack left—and he would leave—he was going to, yet again, own all her heart. If he didn't already...

Molly walked over to his desk, surprised that

he'd yet to hear or sense her. He was in the zone, she realized, concentrating so deeply that he'd shut out the world.

Amused, Molly tiptoed into the space next to his chair, bent down and ran her hand down his chest.

Mack's head jerked back, missed her nose and caught her cheek in a glancing blow. Molly released a quick hiss of pain, more surprised than hurt.

Molly held her cheek, breathing deeply. Mack stood up and gently peeled her fingers away from her face. "Mol, are you okay? Jesus, I didn't know you were there. What the hell were you thinking sneaking up on me?"

Molly winced as his fingers prodded the area on her cheekbone his hard head connected with. "Ow, dammit."

"I don't think it will bruise but maybe we should get you some ice," Mack said, his expression grim.

The pain was already fading and Molly waved his suggestion away. "I'm fine. It's not that bad."

Mack raised one eyebrow. "Are you sure?" he asked, his lips gently touching her cheek as if to kiss it better.

"Very." Molly turned her head to drag her lips against his. "Let's try this again… Morning, Mack."

Mack smiled, his dark eyes tender. "Morning, Curls. Did you enjoy your late start?"

"So much. Thanks for letting me sleep," Molly replied. She lifted her hand to touch his jaw, saw his concern and smiled. "I'm fine, Mack, really. And you're right. I shouldn't have snuck up on you."

Mack placed his hands on either side of the desk and kissed the side of her mouth, gently moving his lips across hers in a kiss that was sexy as it was sweet. It was an "I missed you" kiss, a "hi, there" smooch.

Completely perfect.

When Mack pulled back, Molly remembered his earlier jumpiness. "What on earth are you working on that held your complete attention? I could've set off a bomb in here and you wouldn't have heard a damn thing."

Mack took a step back, then another and, before her eyes, he morphed back into being the supersuccessful businessman, the tough-as-nails negotiator. As his eyes darkened, her heart sank.

"There's a problem, Molly." He nodded to one of the visitors' chairs. "Take a seat."

Molly stiffened at his suddenly cold tone, his bleak eyes. Her cheek forgotten, she walked around the desk and perched on the edge of the seat, pressing her knees together. She knew, from a place deep inside her, that whatever came out of Mack's mouth next would crack their shaky foundation.

"You're starting to scare me, Mack," Molly said when he didn't speak. "Is it Jameson? Has he taken a turn for the worse?"

"No." Mack turned his computer and tapped his keyboard before placing his hands flat on the desk, his expression intense. "As you know, I've been trying to make sense of Moonlight Ridge's accounting system—"

Molly grimaced. "The books are in such a mess, I know. I've been pushing Jameson to hire an outside accounting firm but I haven't gotten anywhere. Maybe you can talk him into doing that or, since you have power of attorney, you could just get it done."

Mack stood up and folded his arms across his chest. "Grey has been tasked with hiring an accountant."

"That's a great idea," Molly replied. When Mack's hard expression didn't change, she frowned. "Why do I think there's still something you aren't telling me?"

Mack hauled in a deep breath. "Grey is hiring a forensic accountant, Molly, because a considerable amount of money has been siphoned from the company."

Molly felt the room spin and Mack's tall figure faded in and out. This could not be happening to her, not now. Any minute now Mack would tell her he was joking and, after he did, she would, without a doubt, punch him.

She knew he liked to tease but this was, well, hurtful and…cruel.

Mack was impatient and a hard ass, sometimes ruthless; she'd never thought him to be cruel.

"Mack, that's not funny!" Molly stated, her voice trembling with rage.

"I. Am. Not. Joking." Mack elucidated every word, his voice deep and hard and so very intimidating.

Molly closed her eyes, hoping that when she opened them this would be a bad dream. Forcing herself to look at him, she wrapped her arms around herself, hoping to melt the icy core that was growing inside her. "God, you really aren't. How much?"

"I'm not sure yet. We need a forensic accountant to get an accurate figure. But at least tens of thousands of dollars."

"God." Molly lifted her hands to her lips as if she was praying. "But how?"

Mack stared at her, his expression resolute. "Shouldn't you be asking who, Molly?"

Of course, but she didn't want to go there. The people who were in the position to steal money were her friends, people she'd worked with for years and years.

"Look, Beth has horrible taste in men but she pushes paper, she doesn't sign any checks or anything. Fern, our exec chef has worked here for more than two decades. Harry has been here forever. Ross doesn't have a long history with us but Jameson and I both trust him. Our staff is loyal, Mack. They wouldn't have done this."

"You left someone out, Molly."

"Who?" Molly demanded, running over her list. No, she hadn't; not really. Those were the only people who dealt with paperwork, who could pull off some illicit scheme.

"You, Molly."

At his two-word sentence, her world as she knew, cracked and crumbled.

"You, Molly."

Mack kept his eyes on hers, watched as shock consumed her features and her knees wobbled. Her irises dilated and he could hear the harsh sounds of her irregular breathing. He knew that if he put his hands on her skin, she would be clammy and cold and her hand pressing into her stomach suggested that she was feeling nauseated.

As if she'd heard his silent thought, Molly's eyes darted around the room. "I think I'm going to be sick."

Mack bent down to pick up the trash basket and thrust it under her nose. Molly bent over the basket, heaved and he winced when she expelled her coffee into the trash receptacle.

It wasn't pretty, it wasn't nice—some would even call him cruel—but yeah, he needed to get her immediate response...

Mack glanced at the small camera within his state-of-the-art laptop, which he'd angled to point in her direction. Its flashing light told him it was still recording.

He'd spent another few hours in this office last night, running through what he did and didn't know, what he suspected and what he could prove. Despite his earlier, and brief doubts, he absolutely knew Molly wasn't the thief but what he knew and could prove were very different.

And the real thief had done, on the surface at least, a damn fine job at pointing the finger at her…

He needed to control the situation but more than that, he needed to protect her. It was, after all, what he did.

Moonlight Ridge was an Asheville institution and Jameson was one of the city's favorite citizens. He'd also been a source of good copy—starting with inheriting the place from the billionaire Tip O'Sullivan when he was in his early thirties. He'd been regarded as an extremely eligible bachelor and speculation was rife as to who would wear his ring. Instead of producing a wife, he fostered, then adopted, three boys, raising eyebrows. Molly's father's embezzlement caused an uproar, and Jameson's recent ill health made headlines again.

Jameson was interesting and the reporters would be all over this new drama. When news of the theft became common knowledge, and he had no doubt it would, fingers would be pointed in Molly's direction. She had access to the inn's bank account; she was in the position to steal from him; she was her father's daughter.

And, because the Haskell family couldn't keep their damn mouths shut—Grant's pillow talk with Beth was a great example—the world would soon know Molly stole money from his dad when she was a scared teen.

The press would eviscerate her unless he protected her. He could shout it from the rooftops that Molly was innocent but everyone at Moonlight Ridge knew they were sleeping together and his defense of her would mean nothing. No, Molly was her own best defense.

If it became necessary—when the reporters started circling, or the police came calling—he could show them a video of her unfiltered, instinctive response.

No one who saw her reaction, her shock and physical reaction to being accused, would doubt her innocence. Protecting and loving Molly was what he was put on this earth to do and this, unfortunately, was the best way he could.

It was a temporary pain for a long-term solution. This way he'd be in control of the narrative…

Molly finally dropped the basket, her face white. Mack quickly walked across the room to the bar fridge in the corner and pulled out a bottle of water, cracking the top and holding the bottle for her to take.

He expected her to take it, to drink some water to remove the foul taste in her mouth, and to sink to the chair.

Instead of doing that, any of it, Molly slapped the open water bottle from his hand. When her eyes connected with his, he realized that her blistering anger coated soul-deep hurt. "You son of a bitch! How dare you accuse me of stealing from Jameson? Especially after what I told you about what I did and how guilty I feel."

Mack winced. Yeah, explaining his actions wasn't going to be easy. Or any fun at all.

Mack picked up a small remote off his desk, the one that controlled the camera, his finger on the pause button. But he needed one more reaction from her; one sentence that was a decent denial, hopefully bellowed at the top of her voice. "How much did you steal from Jameson, Molly?"

Molly, her temper erupting, picked up a stapler from his desk and hurled it at his head. "I didn't steal a damn thing, you prick! I don't know what you are talking about and I'm gutted that you think that I had. How dare you think I would do that?"

Good enough, Mack thought, cutting the recording. Now it was time to do some damage control, to make Molly understand that he'd led her down this rocky and thorny path to help, not hurt her.

But judging by her heaving chest and flamethrower eyes, that was going to be harder than he anticipated.

"Sit down, sweetheart."

This time an empty coffee cup flew past his head, narrowly missing his ear. Her aim, dammit, was getting better.

"Don't you dare call me sweetheart, you two-faced pile of cockroach vomit!"

Mack winced.

"I know that you didn't steal the money, Molly!"

Mack bellowed. She stared at him, her mouth falling open.

"What?"

He held up the remote in his hand, quickly explaining that he'd recorded her reaction, that he'd defy anyone to think she was guilty after seeing the footage.

"This is so bad. I cannot believe this is happening," Molly whispered, her voice breaking.

"It'll be okay, Molly. I believe in you. We'll fight this, together."

"The hell we will."

Mack frowned at her response, thinking that he was missing something here. She wasn't reacting anything like he'd expected her to.

Molly gripped the back of the chair with white fingers, staring down at the floor. When she finally lifted her face, Molly's eyes were dry and, at that moment Mack realized her pain was too deep for tears. She lifted her index finger, cocking her head to the side.

"Question…instead of this crazy scheme, why didn't you sit me down, tell me what was happening and let us come up with a plan to prove my innocence together?"

Uh…good question.

"Fifteen years ago you left my life because *you* decided, without consulting me, that was the best for me. You've just done that, *again*. Who gave you the right to take control, to find a solution and to make decisions without me?" Molly's intense eyes stood out in her still-white face. "How dare you!"

Whoa, wait, hold on…

But before he could respond, words started flying out of Molly's mouth. "I am not a child. Nor am I a ditsy girl who needs you to make decisions for me. You arrogant bastard! This is *my* life, *my* reputation and *my* career. If I am being accused of theft then I will fight it. I will react and respond the way *I* feel is right!"

"I was trying to help you," Mack protested.

"No, you were trying to control the situation and control *me*," Molly replied, her tone bitter. "I've come to terms with you leaving me then. I can forgive that young and stupid boy, but you treating me like this, it's unacceptable, Holloway. It's hurtful and disrespectful, controlling— I said that already—and incredibly patronizing. I thought that maybe there was something building between us again, something wonderful and worthwhile. But you don't love *me*, you love the girl you used to know, the one you used to protect. You don't see the woman I am today, the one who is capable and smart and determined and independent."

"I—"

"Don't you dare say a word." Molly whipped out the words, cutting him off. "You've lost the right to take part in this conversation! I have lived my life without your help and guidance for fifteen years and I think I've done okay. So, screw you and screw your need to control everybody and everything."

"I'm better off on my own, I always have been. Thanks for the reminder." Molly turned to walk toward the door, her back stiff and straight.

"Jesus, Molly, will you listen to me?" Mack bellowed, not knowing what he would say if she gave him even half a chance.

Molly just shook her head and walked away from him. And Mack knew that, in his cockiness, in his hastily concocted need-to-control-everything plan, he'd gone too far. He'd hurt her, badly.

And while Molly had an enormous heart, she wasn't stupid and she tended not to repeat past mistakes so she'd never love him now and she'd never trust him again.

He was—what was the word he was looking for?—screwed.

Ten

Later that afternoon Mack left yet another message on Molly's voice mail system. "Dammit, Molly, call me! It's about Jameson. He's back in the hospital."

Giada placed a hand in the center of his back and Mack looked down at the tiny woman standing next to him. He could see his fear reflected in her eyes, and Mack pushed a fist into his sternum as he dropped into one of the plastic seats in the hospital waiting room.

"I can't get a hold of her." Mack dropped his head, his forearms on his thighs. "She needs to be here."

With him. Because that was where she belonged. He needed her, craved her, loved her and he wanted her by his side riding every wave life sent their way. The small ripples, breakers that could be easily surfed, the storm-whipped monster waves.

He could live his life on his own, taking his chances, but he didn't want to. He wanted to share his journey with Molly. As a team, a partnership, equal in every way.

And he wanted everything with the woman who was not currently speaking to him. And might never again.

In the hours between Molly's storming out of his office and Giada's frantic call, he'd examined his actions and had a couple of come-to-Jesus moments. As hard as it was to admit, Molly had been entitled to rip six layers of skin off him. She wasn't a child; his actions had been high-handed and the I'll-protect-you dynamic that characterized their childhood didn't apply anymore.

Molly wanted, and deserved, someone who respected and valued her input. If she ever forgave him, he'd never forget the lessons he learned today.

The phone in his hand buzzed and Mack hit

the green button without looking to see who was calling. "Mol?"

"No, it's me… Grey."

Mack rubbed his fingers across his forehead. He'd left messages for his brothers, telling them Giada found Jameson on the floor of his bedroom, conscious but mentally confused.

"How is Pops, Mack?" Grey demanded.

"They think it might be a stroke but the tests will confirm that. If it is, then they can treat him immediately and he'll have a great chance of recovery," Mack told his brother.

"And if it's another bleed?"

That was a question Mack didn't want to answer. "Let's just wait and see, bro. Are you on your way?"

Grey told him that he was boarding his flight and would be with him in a few hours. Mack disconnected the call and his phone rang again. He felt the same flare of hope that it was Molly but it was Travis. After a brief conversation with him and confirming that he was also en route to Asheville, Mack tried Molly again, to no avail.

"I can't get a hold of her," he told Giada again.

"You will." Giada patted his hand. Her eyes

went to the door, willing a doctor to walk into the room to give them some news.

As if she manifested him, a small woman walked into the room, a satisfied smile on her face. Both Mack and Giada sprang to their feet, anxious for news.

"Mr. Holloway is fine," she told him.

"He didn't have a stroke or a brain bleed?" Giada demanded, her voice shrill with anxiety.

"Nope. We ran the tests, did an MRI and we can't see anything that indicates a serious neurological event."

Mack's heart rate dropped to a more regular rhythm and he took his first full breath in what felt like years.

"Come with me." Dr. Bell gestured them to follow her, which they did, Mack following a step behind the two small women.

Dr. Bell led them into a private room and Mack looked over to the bed, where his father sat, resting on a mound of pillows. He glared at Giada and then at Mack. "Get me the hell out of here," he growled.

Mack smiled. If Jameson was feeling uncooperative, then he would be fine.

"We want you to stay overnight for observation. I'm sure you will be able to go home tomorrow," Dr. Bell told him, not at all intimidated by his gruff father.

Mack walked up to Jameson and dropped a kiss on his bald head, smiling when Jameson told him to stop being sloppy. But he saw the tiny smile on Jameson's face, the hint of pleasure. Yeah, his dad was still a sucker for affection.

Mack folded his arms and looked at the doctor. He was about to ask what caused his setback when Molly ran into the room, her face blotchy and red, her eyes frantic.

She immediately rushed over to Jameson and threw herself onto his chest, burying her face in his neck. "You can't die, dammit! I won't let you! I need you, Jameson."

Jameson's big hand curled around the back of Molly's head and his eyes cut to Mack's face, his expression as black as thunder. He could easily read the silent demand in his eyes. *What the hell did you do to her?*

Yep, Molly was definitely his favorite child, the one who could do no wrong. And really, since she was his favorite person in the whole world, he had no problem with that.

Giada, calm and practical, rubbed her hand over Molly's back, just like she'd done to him earlier. "Jameson is fine, darling. Dr. Bell wants to tell us what she discovered."

Molly stood up slowly, wiped the tears from her eyes with a tissue Giada handed her and slid her hand into Jameson's.

She hadn't once looked at him since she'd run into the room. He was all but invisible. It was clear that Molly had cut him out of her life. And, really, he couldn't blame her.

He'd been given a second chance with her and he'd blown it. Badly. Because he was a control freak moron.

Molly looked at Dr. Bell. "So what put him in the hospital?"

Dr. Bell jammed her hands into the pockets of her white coat. "As I said, the MRI scan and the tests we did showed no neurological issues. I think Mr. Holloway is looking good, brain-wise."

"That's up for debate," Giada quipped. Mack frowned, wondering if he was imagining the flirtatious smile she sent Jameson. But maybe, because he had love on his mind, he was imagining something that wasn't there. And, let's be honest, he didn't think he could cope with Jameson and Giada acting like besotted teenagers.

Though, given their combative personalities, any romance between them would be full of sarcasm and snark.

Anyway, that wasn't important. Not right now.

"Mr. Holloway, I consulted with my colleagues and we all agree you had a reaction to the new drug we prescribed for you. One of its side effects is confusion and instability."

"Then why did you prescribe it?" Molly demanded, her voice irate. Yeah, she'd go to war for Jameson.

When Molly loved, she loved hard and fiercely and with everything she had. He needed that, for himself, and for the family he wanted to create with her. Because there had only ever been Molly, would only be her.

Dr. Bell shrugged. "It's effective for managing seizures and that's what we are trying to prevent. But there are other drugs as effective and I'll prescribe those instead. They have fewer side effects."

"Maybe that's what you should've given him in the first place," Molly told her, chin up and green fire blazing from her red-rimmed eyes.

Giada rubbed her arm. "Everyone's body chemistry is different and reactions to medicine can differ from patient to patient. Dr. Bell is doing the best she can, Molly dear."

Molly's expression clearly stated her disagreement with Giada's statement.

"I know that you would like to be at home, Mr. Holloway, but as I said, I'd prefer it if you stayed the night," Dr. Bell said, ignoring Molly.

"He'll stay," Molly and Giada chimed at the same time.

Jameson rolled his eyes at Mack, who just lifted a shoulder in a "what can you do?" shrug. He wasn't brave enough to take on Molly and Giada at the same time and, when Jameson's shoulders slumped, realized his father wasn't up to the task, either.

As Dr Bell left the room, Jameson turned his attention to Molly. "You've been crying," he accused.

Molly swatted a curl away. "That's what happens when I get a million calls telling me you are back in the hospital."

Jameson narrowed his eyes at her. "That's not why you were crying."

Molly mustered up a smile. "I'm fine, Jameson. I promise."

Jameson's frown deepened as he looked from Molly to Mack and back again. "Look, I know you are all trying to keep me wrapped up in cotton wool but I won't have it! What is going on?"

They'd been told to keep his anxiety levels down and that was what they'd do. Judging by Molly's attempt to smile, she agreed. They both loved Jameson and would do anything in their power to shield him from stress.

Jameson slapped his hands on his thighs. "I demand to know what made you cry."

Molly's frantic eyes met his and he caught the small shake of her head. They were on the same page; she wanted to keep the embezzlement at Moonlight Ridge quiet.

"If one of you doesn't start talking, I'm going to get out of bed and beat it out of you," Jameson told them. Mack recognized it for the idle threat it was since Jameson never once raised a hand to any of them.

"Pops, just relax. We're handling everything," Mack said, trying to soothe him.

"I don't want you to handle it. I want to be involved. I want to know what's going on!"

Jameson shouted, gripping the bed covers with a tight hold.

Mack winced. Jameson, whenever he got the bit between his teeth, refused to let go. He'd yell and shout until he got an answer. And if they tried to leave, he was stubborn enough to follow them out the door.

They had to tell him something…something he'd believe.

But Mack didn't know what.

Molly took the decision out of his hands by sitting on the bed facing Jameson, her thigh next to his hip. Mack knew she was going to confess and he wished she wouldn't; not because Jameson couldn't take it but because he didn't want to alter the relationship between Jameson and Molly.

"Mol, *don't.*"

Molly didn't drop her eyes from Jameson's face. "I have to, Mack. I can't live with it anymore and he deserves to know."

Jameson's huge hand covered Molly's, making hers disappear from view. "Is this about the two grand you stole when you were a kid?" he asked.

Molly's mouth dropped open, the shock causing her features to slacken. Mack was better at masking his emotions but he felt his eyes widen. So the old man knew all along? What the hell? Mack looked at Giada, who didn't look too surprised, either. She hadn't been around at the time so that meant Jameson told her.

How close were these two anyway?

"You know?" Molly whispered.

"I've known since the day you took it."

"But...how?"

Jameson shrugged. "It wasn't hard to figure out. You were the only person besides the boys who knew I stashed money in that Chinese tea caddy."

"Everyone knew you did that, Jay," Giada told him.

Jameson rolled his eyes at her. "Okay then, smarty-pants, Molly was the only person who knew, had access to my office and who was in a jam."

Mack leaned his shoulder into the wall and dropped his head to hide his smile. Damn, the old man was sharp. And how stupid were they to think that they'd pulled one over on him? He always knew everything...

A tear ran down Molly's cheek. "I'm so, so sorry. I know it was wrong but—"

"But you were being evicted and your family made it your problem to find the money," Jameson said, sounding disgusted. "You were a kid, Molly. They had no right to put pressure on you to find a solution."

"Still, I stole from you," Molly said, her voice breaking. "I have the money. I put it into a savings account and its earned interest. I'll write you a check." Molly pulled her hand from Jameson's and stood up, her body shaking with tension. "Why didn't you say something?"

Jameson pulled a face. "I kept expecting you to admit it. You never could keep a secret. I nearly told you when you refused my offer to pay for your college expenses—you are stupidly stubborn by the way—"

"I learned it from you," Molly shot back.

"I expected you to tell me when you first started working for me but you didn't. So I respected your privacy and decided that you would tell me when you were ready. Or you might not. Either way, it didn't change how much I loved you, how proud I was of you."

Molly dropped her head and stared at the floor. "How can you say that? I did what my father did. I stole from you."

For the first time Mack saw the anger in Jameson's eyes, but quickly realized it wasn't directed at Molly but at her father. "Your father was an adult, who chose to steal to fund his gambling habit. I offered him help. He chose to steal from me instead. The only person in your family who understood the gravity of his crimes was you, Molly. You were so young but you instinctively knew the difference between right and wrong. Your family, not so much."

Jameson patted the space next to him and when Molly sat down, he cupped her cheek with his broad, gentle hand. Mack swallowed, touched by the tenderness in his father's eyes. "It was such a bad time, Mol, and I was off my game. I focused all my attention on Travis and I neglected my other boys."

Jameson's eyes connected with Mack's and he saw the deep and intense apology within those dark depths. Mack acknowledged his apology with a nod and a small smile.

And in one look, Mack released that his past was over and it was time to create a better, brighter future.

Jameson looked at Molly. "I neglected you, too, Molly darling. I know that you felt lost and alone. I'd heard your family was in financial trouble again and I paid the rent for six months a week or two before you took the money. Because I was juggling so many balls in the air, I forgot to tell you.

"But you should've come to me, Molly," he added, his voice a little stern.

"I know. But you had your own family stuff going on—"

Jameson released an irritated growl. "You are a part of my family, Molly. You always have been. From the moment your father died, you became mine. Not in a legal sense, but here." Jameson thumped his chest, his eyes bright with unshed tears. "And you should've confessed a long time ago."

Molly sucked her bottom lip between her pretty teeth. "I know. I'm so sorry."

"So you should be," Jameson grumbled. He crooked his finger at her. "Come here, baby girl."

Molly dropped back down to the bed and rested her head on his chest, her closed eyes leaking tears. Mack looked at Giada, who was dabbing at her own eyes with a tissue. His eyes were also, annoyingly, damp.

Mack walked over to the window and stared

down into the parking lot below, his thoughts whirling. Jameson and Molly would be fine but he wasn't fool enough to believe she'd forgive him that easily. But now that they knew his dad would be fine, his only goal was to win Molly back.

He wanted, needed, her in his life, in his bed, as the mother of his children. Because frankly, he couldn't conceive of a life without her in it. He'd only existed the past fifteen years, but over the past two months, he'd lived and laughed and loved.

This was going to be the fight of his life and winning her back was all that mattered.

Molly left the hospital feeling mentally exhausted and physically drained. But knowing this dreadful day couldn't get much worse, she decided to head across town to confront her family, to end her relationship with them…

Permanently.

From her seat behind the wheel of her car, Molly stared at the small house she'd purchased for her mom, noticing the grass lawn hadn't been cut for a while or the shutters repainted. Vincent's truck sat in the driveway, a trickle of fresh oil running down the pavement. A rusted bicycle still sat under the tree, as it had for the past ten years, maybe more.

She didn't belong here. These weren't her people. Oh, not because they were poor but because they refused to *try*. Because they'd always take the easy way out, they couldn't stop playing the victim and because they made such damn awful decisions.

And because they routinely lied to her. And used her.

Molly left her car and walked up the cracked path to the door. On hearing an expensive engine, she turned and sighed when she saw Mack's Mercedes pull up behind her car.

She couldn't deal with him now. Or, possibly, ever.

Molly glared at him as he approached her. "What are you doing here?" she demanded. Then she waved her question away. "I don't actually care. Just go away, Mack."

"There is no way I'm going to let you confront your family alone. I told you that before and it still holds."

"How did you know I was going to be here?"

"I know you, Molly. I knew that when you left the hospital, this would be your first stop."

He knew her? Really? What rubbish! "Yet, you don't know me well enough to talk to me when a problem arises, to work with me to find a solution. No, you thought you could just charge in and make decisions for me like I'm an incompetent idiot!"

Before Mack could respond, the front door opened. "Will you two please stop yelling? Vince is asleep."

Molly stepped onto the porch and addressed her mom. "Then I suggest you wake him up, Mom. We're going to have a talk and I'm not leaving until I've said what I need to."

"You can't just come over here and make demands," Grant told her, his face contorted into an ugly sneer. He pushed past Vivi to step onto the small porch.

Mack stepped forward, putting himself between Molly and her brother. "She can do whatever the hell she wants to since she's the one funding this suckfest. Go get your brother because, by God, if I have to haul him out of bed, he'll regret it. So will you."

Molly had never seen such a cold, hard expression on Mack's face and when Grant disappeared back into the house, she knew her brother felt it was prudent not to argue.

A few minutes later Vincent, half-asleep, joined them on the porch. Her mom, looking anxious, gestured for them to go inside. Molly shook her head. This last conversation could take place on the porch.

"So I found out something quite interesting today," she said when she had their attention. And, as annoying as he was, she was glad to have Mack standing next to her.

The next few minutes wouldn't be pleasant.

"What would that be?" Grant snidely asked.

"I found that you never needed the money I stole from Jameson. He'd already paid the rent." Her eyes darted from her mom's face to Vincent's, to Grant's and then back to her mom's. Nobody rushed to deny her words; nor were they shocked by her statement. Molly felt fury bubble up her throat. "I was seventeen and I didn't want to take the money. You all told me that if I didn't, we'd be evicted. Yet the rent had been paid, for several months."

Molly felt Mack's hand on her back and immediately felt steadier, more in control. She slapped her hands on her hips, keeping her attention on her mother. "You've blackmailed me for years! Why would you do that to me?"

Vivi shrugged. "Jameson had money. We didn't. And he caused your father's death and took away our only source of income."

"Dad stole from him, Mom!" Molly yelled. "Do you not get that?"

Another shrug. "Jameson was adamant that he wouldn't drop the charges. If he'd just let your father resign, he could've landed a job and we wouldn't be here, living in this crappy house."

"A house you didn't pay for! A house I bought, with the money I worked my ass off to make. What have any of you done?" Molly shouted.

"Sponged off you," Mack said, his tone withering.

"You manipulated me, played me, let me believe something that wasn't true for all these years and I will never, ever forgive you for doing that," Molly said, her voice cracking. "Why would you do that? I'm your daughter, your sister."

Vivi snorted. "You were your daddy's girl and then when he died, you attached yourself to Jameson."

"Because he, at least, seemed to love me," Molly shouted.

Mack placed his hand on her shoulder and gently squeezed. Molly leaned into him, just for a minute. It felt so damn good to lean, to soak in his support. But then she remembered what he'd done and reminded herself that she didn't need him, just like she didn't need her family.

She was better off alone.

Molly lifted her hands, palms out, in a just-stop gesture. "I'm done. Don't ever contact me again."

"But—"

Molly forced herself to look at her mother. "But what?"

Vivi gestured to the house. "What are you going to do about this house? It's in your name but you gave it to me."

Why was she surprised at the lack of reaction, of feeling? Why was she shocked by her mom putting herself first?

"I'll sign it over to you," Molly said, feeling completely wiped out. "Do what you want with it. Just don't ever call me again."

Vincent and Grant exchanged a long look and Molly knew that they weren't done with her yet.

"Then what about a goodbye present, sis? Something to wish us well as you leave our lives?" Grant asked, his eyes dancing with maliciousness. "We still need that ten grand for my new business."

God, you couldn't make up crap like this. Shaking her head, she turned to walk down the steps, trembling with rage. But not with surprise. Her brothers were the ultimate scavengers, after all.

Molly heard a hard smack and whirled around, just in time to see Grant sliding down the wall next to the front door, blood flowing from his obviously broken nose. Vincent, ever loyal, jumped on Mack's back but was easily dislodged with a jab of Mack's elbow to his gut, quickly followed by a punch to his kidneys. Vincent followed Grant to the floor.

It was all over in ten seconds.

Vivi released a harsh cry as she took in her white-faced sons. "I'll press charges," she told Mack. "I'll have you arrested for assault."

Mack just handed her a cold, hard-as-steel smile. "Your threats don't scare me, Vivi. They never have. Do not contact Molly. Do not let your sons contact her. No text messages, no emails, no visits. If any of you come within a mile of her, I will destroy you." He smiled again and Molly shivered. "Are we clear?"

Vivi, her hand to her throat, nodded.

Mack joined Molly on the path and placed a hand on her lower back and urged her forward. As they walked to their cars, Beth stepped onto the path, looking vaguely amused.

"Ooh, drama. And damn, it looks like I missed it," she said. Then she caught sight of Vincent and Grant on the floor of the small porch, Grant's shirt splattered with blood.

"What the hell happened?" she demanded.

Mack kept moving Molly forward. "You can get the story from them. Oh, and, Beth?"

"What?" Beth asked, glaring at him.

"You're fired."

Despite being furious with Mack and feeling sick and sad from her encounter with her family, Molly silently cheered his blunt declaration.

Beth sneered at him. "You can't fire me because I am sleeping with your girlfriend's brother."

"I'm not. I'm firing you because you are a piss-poor bookkeeper. Don't bother to collect your final check. I'll have it delivered."

"But...but...you can't!" Beth wailed.

"I just did." Mack's mouth lifted at the edges in the tiniest of smiles. "Jameson always used to tell us that if you lie down with dogs, you get up with fleas. My advice to you? Disinfect."

Mack didn't bother to follow Molly home. He knew exactly where she was going and when he saw her car parked in the space next to the road leading to the steel bridge, he drove his car to the villa and parked it in the garage.

He slowly made his way down the road toward the steel bridge and, ultimately, to the pond and the treehouse where he knew Molly would be.

It was her thinking place, their special place. But as much as he wanted to be with her, he also knew she needed a little time to calm down, to pull herself together.

He'd give her some time but before the sun set, they'd have an understanding between them.

He wasn't leaving her life again; he'd never underestimate her or try to control her again. And he was prepared to spend the rest of his life proving that to her.

Mack heard his ringing phone and pulled the device out of the back pocket of his khakis, knowing he couldn't ignore his father's call. He swiped the green button and his father's face filled his screen.

"How did it go? Have you two kissed and made up yet?" Jameson demanded.

"Stop bugging me or I'll tell Giada that you keep a secret stash of cigars in the inside pocket of your winter coat," Mack retorted.

Mack heard Giada's triumphant shout and Jameson scowled. "Dammit, Mack! You have a very big mouth."

Jameson turned the phone and Mack saw that his dad wasn't alone in his hospital room. Travis and Grey, trying hard to ignore each other, stood on either side of Jameson, while Giada sat in the visitor's chair, glee on her face.

"You shouldn't be smoking anyway," Mack told Jameson.

"Yada yada," Jameson said. "Did she confront her family?"

Mack nodded. "Yeah, she did. It was pretty ugly."

"They are ugly people," Jameson agreed.

"How many Haskell brothers did you deck, Mack?" Grey asked.

"Both of them." Mack looked down at his swollen knuckles, suddenly conscious of the insistent throbbing in his hand. Worth it, he decided.

Silence fell between them and Mack sighed, over it. This couldn't go on. Molly, obviously, was his top priority, but getting his family back ran a close second.

Stopping, he stared down at the screen, noticing that Travis had turned away to look out the window and that Grey was staring at his own phone. Nobody was talking to each other and he was over it.

He was so done with this cold war.

"I have a few things to say," Mack stated, determined. When Travis didn't turn around, Mack sighed. "Travis, look at me, dammit."

His brother resumed his place behind Jameson's shoulder, his scowl telling him he didn't appreciate his barked order. Mack didn't much care. "About our conversation last night, we were wrong to even consider that possibility."

"What are you talking about?" Jameson demanded.

He wouldn't explain but Grey and Travis knew that he was referring to Molly's innocence. "Are you sure?" Grey asked.

"Very," Mack emphatically stated. Grey nodded, accepting his word, but on seeing Travis's hesitance, Mack spoke again. "I need you to trust me on this, Trav. Please."

Travis nodded and Mack released a sigh of relief. On his word, his brothers accepted Molly's innocence. The realization both humbled and touched him.

But there was more to say and Mack spoke before Jameson could demand another explanation for their obscure conversation.

"I'm done with this cold war between us. I miss my family," Mack told his siblings. "I'm so sorry I lost control of the vehicle. I'm still gutted that you were injured, Trav. I'm also gutted that you lost your football scholarship and that you never got to play pro ball. I fully accept all responsibility for the accident."

Grey looked like he was about to speak but Mack's hard look stopped whatever he'd been planning to say. "I'm also sorry for running instead of sticking and staying. But it's been fifteen years, dammit."

Mack rubbed the back of his neck, tasting tears in the back of his throat. "Fifteen years of not being able to grab a beer, a late-night chat, of not being able to tease you, talk you down or talk you up. Fifteen years of not talking and I'm goddamn sick of it!" Mack shouted, the dam bursting on his carefully held back emotions. "You're my brothers and I don't care what I have to do but we *will* be a family again."

Travis shook his head. "We can't just go back, Mack. It doesn't work like that."

"I don't want to go back, Travis. I want to go forward," Mack told him. "Give me a chance. Give us a chance."

Travis lifted and dropped his massive shoulders. "I don't know. Maybe."

From his stubborn-ass brother, a *maybe* was a very good place to start and more than he expected. Mack smiled at him. "I'm gonna wear you down."

A smile touched his eyes. "You can try."

Mack, feeling lighter, just managed to stop himself from doing an air punch.

"So does this mean I can host a Sunday lunch this weekend?" Jameson demanded.

On cue, Mack and his brothers shuddered and groaned. Jameson wasn't a great cook and his roast duck was always burned on the outside and raw on the inside.

They exchanged anxious looks and Mack finally nodded. "I'll be around."

"I can fly back on Saturday, stay over and fly back on Sunday evening," Grey said.

Travis rubbed the back of his neck. "I'm not sure I can make it. I have a lot on my plate. I can try."

Mack knew that there was little chance of Travis breaking bread with them on Sunday. He wasn't, he knew, ready to bury the past or to revive family traditions.

"I'll make my famous roast duck." Jameson looked excited. Oh, God. It sounded really awful but he'd eat a hundred awful ducks if it meant having his family back together again.

"You are not nearly well enough to cook," Giada told Jameson, her tone suggesting he not argue. "I will cook. Lunch will be served at one. If you are going to join us, do not be late. Asparagus salad with parmigiana, seafood pasta, tiramisu. Yes?"

"Yes!" Mack and Grey chimed in unison while Travis remained silent.

It would be wonderful, Mack admitted, to spend some time with Grey, but let's be honest here. Sunday lunches wouldn't be the same until all three of them were back in their chairs, eating at their father's table.

Molly knew that Mack would join her at the treehouse, so his sinking into one of the huge cushions on the deck wasn't a surprise.

The fact that he just sat quietly, waiting for her to speak, was. Mack didn't usually hold back; he was in-your-face assertive. But she refused to look at him, refused to try and work out what he was thinking. Along with her family, she was done with him.

Or, more honestly, she *wanted* to be done with him.

Molly rested her chin on her bent knee and stared at the calm waters of the pond, wondering whether she should stay at Moonlight Ridge or try and forge a path somewhere else. Jameson would understand if she left. He had, after all, encouraged his sons' efforts to fly harder, farther and higher and he'd afford her the same respect and consideration.

A part of her wondered if she could cut it in a competitive environment; wondered if she could hack a corporate culture. Then she remembered that she'd survived thirty-plus years of her family's backbiting and manipulation. She'd be fine.

She was a hard worker, was smart and canny and her BS meter was well tuned. She'd make it anywhere.

But did she want to go? When Mack left—and Molly prayed that would be soon—did she want to stay at Moonlight Ridge, help Grey and then Travis, discover who the real thief was? She rather thought that she did. She was, after all, being set up to take the fall. She wanted to help nail the perp's hide to the wall. And, she adored Moonlight Ridge. It was her place and she was the best person to manage it.

But that meant working and dealing with the oldest Holloway brother, for a few more weeks at least. "When are you going back to Nashville?"

Mack considered her harsh question before answering her. "Grey is taking over from me soon, I do need to get back on the road so that'll suit me."

Mid-June was just ten days away; she could tolerate him for that long, surely? She'd have to...

"But I'm seriously thinking of relocating my

Nashville headquarters to Asheville," Mack added.

Molly banged her forehead on her knee. Why was life punishing her like this? "Why?"

"I want to be around more, hang out with Jameson, bug Grey. And, when it's Travis's turn to look after the resort, I want to spend some time with him, too," Mack said, his voice even.

"Making amends, Holloway?" Molly demanded.

"Yeah. But that's not the biggest bridge I need to rebuild."

Molly didn't pretend to misunderstand him. "Good luck with that."

She could see the remorse in his eyes, his expression frustrated. "I messed up, Molly, I know that. I absolutely should've brought my concerns to you before going off half-cocked."

"Did you suspect me of taking the money?" Molly demanded. "Even once?"

"Yes," Mack replied, his expression grave.

She thought she'd be angrier but she respected his blunt admission of the truth.

"And no..."

Well, that was a confusing answer. Molly raised her eyebrows in a silent command to explain.

"Maybe a part of me wanted you to be guilty because then I could go back to my boring, staid and uneventful life. Maybe I was looking for a way to put distance between us. There's a chance that I chose to act like I did because I knew it would infuriate you and you'd call it."

"Congratulations. You succeeded in getting me to do what you wanted," Molly stated, her tone flat.

"But that's not what I want, Mol." Mack stretched his legs out, crossing his feet at the ankles and resting his weight on his arms. "The real reason I didn't want to come back to Asheville was because I knew I wouldn't be able to resist you, Curls."

Molly scoffed at that statement but Mack ignored her. "Over the years I didn't engage with you, couldn't spend any time with you because I, subconsciously, maybe even consciously, knew I would fall for you again. And that's exactly what happened."

Mack turned to face her and rested his forearms on his knees. "I'm so in love with you, Molly. And loving you so much scares me. It scares me enough to run because if I run, if you're not around, I can't lose you."

Molly's heart bounced off her chest. "You lost

me once through your own choice and you lost me again because you acted like a controlling ass."

"Noted. Accepted." Mack picked up a twig from the deck and pulled it through his fingers. "Congratulations on confronting your family, Mol, and on confessing to Jameson."

"Thanks," Molly replied, caught off guard by his change of subject.

"You are so much braver than I, sweetheart," Mack stated. "You stand and fight. I—like my sperm donor—tend to run when life gets tough or inconvenient or too real. I did that years ago as a kid, and I'm ashamed to say I was going to do it again."

"You don't need an excuse, Mack. Just leave. I'm giving you permission to go. Trust me, I'll be fine."

"Except that I would rather chew my wrists off than leave you again," Mack softly said. "I want to stay. I want to fight for you, for our happiness, for our future. I want to be brave like you, Mol. I want to dig my heels in and get stubborn. I want to plant roots and a garden, build a relationship and a house with you. I want to earn your forgiveness, wake up with you in my arms, put a ring on your finger, catch our babies as you give birth to them."

"I'm sticking, Mol. And staying," he added.

Molly fought again the rising tide of joy and tried to push down her happiness. "And what if I tell you that you hurt me too badly, *again*, that I'm not interested in anything you want to do, the life you are offering?"

Dismay and fear flashed in his eyes and, for the first time, she saw his vulnerability. He was scared, too, Molly realized. "Until some other guy makes you deliriously happy, slips into your bed and puts a ring on your finger, I'll fight for us, Molly. I'll do anything and everything to win you back, to get you to trust me again."

Molly heard the determination in his voice, awed by the intensity in his gaze. And suddenly, she knew he was speaking the truth, that she was the reason the sun rose and set for him every day.

Could she trust him, one last time? Could she risk her heart again?

Mack kept his eyes on hers, his focused gaze not wavering. "I'll be rock steady, Molly. I'll be there for you, every step of the way. I'll never disappoint you again." He grimaced. "Oh, I'm not saying I'll never mess up, but when it comes to what's important, I won't let you down, Mol. I won't cheat on you, I promise to always listen to you and take your feelings and opinions into consideration. I promise to trust you. I just need you to give me one more chance."

She felt his assurances deep in her soul and believed every one of them. If she wanted him, Mack was prepared to dive all the way in.

And she couldn't resist him.

She shook her head. "No."

Mack's face fell and he turned away but not before she saw the gleam of tears in his fabulous, black-as-the-night eyes. His bottom lip wobbled, just for a second, and his torso slumped.

"You don't need to try and win me back, Holloway. I have been, always will be, yours."

Mack whipped his head up, his mouth falling open in complete shock. "What?"

"Do try and keep up, Holloway," Molly teased. When he just kept staring at her, Molly touched the tips of her fingers to his jaw. "I'm so in love with you, Mack. I've always loved you, all my life, but this is different. Newer, deeper, scarier."

Mack held her fingers against his face. "I

know, darling. I am scared, too. Let's be scared together."

"How scared?" Molly asked.

"Rings-on-our-fingers scared, building-a-house-overlooking-this-pond scared, trying-to-have-a-kid scared."

Molly smiled at him, not feeling the slightest hint of fear. "That's a lot of fear, Holloway."

Mack nodded. "Yeah, but you make me brave, sweetheart. You make me think I can do anything." He touched his lips, gently, reverently, against hers, pulling back to whisper the words she most wanted to hear against her lips. "I love you so damn much. Be mine, Molly."

"I always have been, Mack. Then, now, forever."

* * * * *

LET'S TALK
Romance

For exclusive extracts, competitions and special offers, find us online:

f facebook.com/millsandboon

◎ @millsandboonuk

🐦 @millsandboon

Or get in touch on 0844 844 1351*

For all the latest titles coming soon, visit millsandboon.co.uk/nextmonth